I0715242

MY FAVORITE LEOPARD

A Phoenix Pictures Vault Novella

BRIANNE GILLEN

This is a work of fiction. Names, characters, places, and incidents either are the product of the author's imagination or are used fictitiously. Any resemblance to actual persons, living or dead, events, or locales is entirely coincidental.

My Favorite Leopard: a Phoenix Pictures Vault Novella

Copyright © 2024 by Brianne Gillen

All rights reserved. No part of this book may be reproduced in any form or by any electronic or mechanical means, including information storage and retrieval systems, without written permission from the author, except for the use of brief quotations in a book review.

Edited by: Michele Chiappetta of Two Birds Author Services

Cover Illustration by: Yulia Yemelianova

Cover Layout by: Brianne Gillen

Print ISBN: 978-1-7372403-8-9

E-book ISBN: 978-1-7372403-9-6

Published by Brianne Gillen

www.briannegillen.com

*To all the cats who've befriended me over the years, especially
Bito & Anonymous Neighbor Cat —
I am sorry my allergies prevented me from properly returning your
affection.
I promise, I was mentally snuggling you from a safe distance.*

Chapter One

Hollywood, California
1949

"**L**ove is a luxury I can't afford."

Lina Leonard trailed one long, red fingernail down the bartender's tie, softening her voice to a throaty purr as she continued, "But why don't you come with me, sweetheart. We can spit in love's face together."

"Cut!"

Lina blinked, coming back to herself as Jerry, her director, conferred with the cameraman and her costar rested against the bar. A few of the extras seated throughout the dark, seedy-looking set began chatting quietly to each other.

"Fantastic work, you two," Jerry called out as he made his way over to the lead actors. "We've got everything we need for this scene." He raised his voice to include the rest of the assembled group. "All right, everyone, let's move on to the kitchen fight!"

The entire soundstage erupted into noisy activity, as Lina relaxed.

"We won't need you for the rest of this, Lina. But seriously, excellent stuff today. As always." He smiled warmly.

"Thanks."

"Enjoy the rest of your afternoon. Tomorrow's call sheet should be ready for you within the hour." He clapped a hand on her costar's shoulder. "Can I have a word about that fight choreography before you head back over to makeup?"

"See you boys later," Lina called over her shoulder, exiting the stage and making a beeline for her dressing room.

Her feet were killing her. As much as she appreciated the wardrobe department's efforts to meet her request for leopard-print pumps, the shoes were definitely made for looks rather than comfort. But eager as she was to move her toes again, her haste was also due to her hope that the script for her next picture had been delivered while she was on set.

Several crew members called out compliments on her performance as she passed. She warmed at their sincere praise, even as it felt like the same-old, same-old. She was more than ready for a change.

Not from acting, though. She didn't think she'd ever tire of being paid to play pretend. Lina had made a name for herself in noir films, and she wouldn't trade her run of success for anything. But there were only so many times a gal could play a femme fatale who roped unsuspecting saps into her nefarious plans—or an unsuspecting sap roped into becoming a femme fatale. Either way, it was growing tedious to always "get what was coming" to her.

So she'd taken a chance and asked for the opportunity to branch out here at Phoenix Pictures. Her nerves had nearly gotten the better of her when she approached the studio head, Lois Ashford, but the woman was a fellow actor who understood completely. Much to Lina's delighted surprise, Phoenix's producers already had her in mind for a new comedy—and while still noir-inspired, it was a promising step in the right direction.

And if delivering a performance that would keep this new

momentum going felt like a daunting task, she was determined to meet the challenge.

Lina focused on the satisfying sound of her heels clicking on the concrete to distract from the excited—and slightly anxious—butterflies that flitted through her stomach at merely the thought of the new project.

"Miss Leonard!" A lad in an emerald-green jacket stood, lying in wait outside her trailer. "There's a phone call for you. They've put it through to your dressing room."

"Oh. Thank you." She hoped it was nothing serious. Like her new film being shelved before it got started.

The page leaned in conspiratorially when she neared. "It's long-distance."

Lina fought to suppress her amusement at the awe in the boy's tone. Though she supposed on his salary, long-distance calls were something of a wonder. She settled for a small smile as she thanked him again.

But as she shut herself into the privacy of her room, the implication of his words sank in, eclipsing the relief that it wasn't bad news from the studio. Who would be calling her long-distance? And at her workplace?

Lina let out a small moan when she stepped out of her shoes, thanking the goddesses for plush carpeting as she removed her right earring and picked up the receiver of her telephone. She immediately recognized the greeting of one of her favorite operators on the lot.

"Hi, Irma. They said there's a call for me?"

"Yup. All the way from San Francisco. Here ya go."

A click sounded, and before she could wonder who the hell she knew in San Francisco, a familiar Irish lilt crackled through the line.

"Lina? Hi. It's Alice."

An odd mix of emotions rushed through Lina—warmth toward one of her oldest and dearest friends, certainly. But also the distant unease that always surfaced with any reminder of the life she'd left behind. Lina suddenly wished she'd asked the page to bring her some ginger ale.

She focused on the warmth, trying to infuse it into her voice. "Alice! Hey! The operator said you're in San Francisco?"

A tiny stab of guilt nudged her. For all they were practically sisters, their chosen paths kept them from seeing much of each other, despite the fact that they lived less than an hour apart in southern California. When Alice wasn't on the road, at least.

Alice replied, "I am. What with that big fire they had up here, it's all hands on deck helping with the rescue efforts. There are lots of big and small critters that need us."

"Oh, right. I hadn't thought…"

Alice's soft laugh tinkled like wind chimes. "Of course you hadn't. Why would you?"

"I did leave all of you behind once upon a time."

"Lina." Alice's voice softened. "It was fully your choice to make. And no one's ever begrudged you that choice."

She allowed herself a chuckle. "I guess I just need a reminder every once in a while."

Lina and Alice had grown up outside Dublin, both born into a long line of powerful Celtic women. And while they might be sisters only in spirit, the likelihood of a shared ancestor somewhere in their matrilineal tree was high, given the gift they both possessed.

If one could call the ability to shift at will into a large, wild feline a gift.

At least they could choose their own cat—in Lina's case, a leopard; Alice's, a lynx.

"Happy to oblige," Alice answered. "And I mean it. This isn't a calling for every one of us, and we all know it. Just like we knew *you* were meant to be a big, important movie star."

Lina snorted. "Mum didn't seem too sure of that when I set off for Hollywood."

"Eh, you were sixteen. She was just worried. But we all believed you had it in ya."

Lina swallowed around the lump in her throat. Any more of this and she'd dissolve into a puddle on the spot. "Hey, as much as I appreciate the pep talk, this call must be costing you a fortune."

Alice coughed. "Right. That it is. But it's worth it. Or at least, it will be. I hope. This might be an awkward moment to bring this up, but … I do have a favor to ask you."

The fine hairs on the back of Lina's neck prickled. "What kind of favor?"

"The kind I'd never ask unless it was an extreme emergency, and for which I will owe you big? Possibly for the rest of my life?"

Lina groaned, sinking into the chair in front of her dressing table.

"You know I'd never bring this to you lightly," Alice rushed on. "But like I said, it's all hands up here, and will be for little while, which leaves no one in my territory. Where you happen to be."

Their kind had been appointed by the goddesses—more generations back than anyone could count—as protectors of all cats, big and small. They stepped in occasionally when nature became too chaotic. But more often than not, unfortunately, their duty arose because their fellow humans became the threat.

Those with the most magic to wield—and who chose to heed their calling, unlike Lina—each had a territory to watch over, and Lina had been thrilled when Alice landed a southern California region a few years back.

"Alice. I cannot possibly be your only choice." Even as she said it, she was certain, deep in her gut, that Alice wouldn't ask unless she was.

"It would be really easy, I swear," Alice intoned.

"Would it, truly?"

"Probably?" Her tone didn't exactly inspire confidence. "This area's pretty quiet, on the whole. The zoo doesn't have the most stellar facilities, but the staff there are reliable. Plus, there's a relatively new animal sanctuary in the foothills that's awfully promising."

"Then why do you need me?" Lina wheedled.

"I'd be neglecting my duties if I didn't put something in place for emergencies. And there is a circus in town right now, over in the Valley; you know how dicey they can get." She paused. "Please, Lina? At least consider it?"

That was the trouble. She *was* considering it, even though she'd never before been tempted. Too often, their brand of help came on the heels of suffering, and it pained her tremendously to see the animals in peril in the first place, even if she could alleviate it.

"Al, I don't know. You've got an awful lot of faith that I could handle anything that might come up." She caught her reflection in the mirror, startled to see her hazel eyes sparking more gold than usual. She hoped it was only the lights.

As if reading her mind, Alice replied, "Your magic has always been strong, Lina. Even after you chose not to use it. It's *almost* as strong as mine."

"Modest as ever, I see," Lina joked, and they both snickered. But she sobered all too quickly. "It's been a while since I've even shifted. I'm out of practice."

She could sense Alice's shrug, even over the phone. "So, practice."

Lina huffed. Easy for her to say. Still, she felt her resolve cracking further.

"I'd only need to step in for something that's absolutely, positively necessary?" she asked.

"Absolutely. Positively. Sooo … you'll do it?"

"Oh, I'm going to regret this," she grumbled. "But yes. Fine. I'll do it."

For a feline, Alice made a high-pitched squeal only dogs could've heard. "Lina, you are the very best. I promise, I will make it up to you. Something tremendous. Anything!" She paused for a moment, and Lina could hear commotion in the background. "Listen, I've got to run."

Lina glanced down at herself. "Me too. I should probably get out of this costume soon."

"I won't keep us, then," Alice replied. "But you've got a spare key to my apartment. There's a safe chest on the floor of my bedroom closet; all the instructions you need are inside. And I'll try to phone you again tomorrow in case you have questions."

"How am I supposed to open the safe?"

"It's charmed to unlock with any of our rings. You still have yours, right?"

"Of course."

Lina immediately opened the little drawer in her dressing table. A large, emerald-cut citrine winked up at her from its simple gold setting. All members of their coven of Felidae received a similar stone as children, and most set it in some kind of jewelry when they got older. Though Lina removed hers when in costume, she never took it off otherwise. It was her primary tether to her family. And when it came to magic, however dormant or unused, the unexpected was always possible, so she never wanted to be caught without a lifeline.

"Okay, good." Alice paused for a heavy moment. "Lina, I can't tell you how much this means to me. Thank you."

She found herself smiling. "You're welcome. And don't worry —I will indeed come up with a massive way you can pay me back."

They shared one last laugh before exchanging farewells.

As soon as she replaced the phone in its cradle, Lina let out a long exhale. She wasn't sure if it was a blessing or a curse that she'd finished filming for the day. She'd welcome a distraction from the growing weight of what she'd just agreed to.

At least she could start with her wardrobe; she quickly changed out of the slinky black dress, swapping it for her own charcoal gray skirt and matching sweater. She secured her favorite leopard-print belt around her waist—her go-to choice for a bit of flair and a jolt of luck—and stepped into a modest, stylish but much comfier pair of heels.

Last, but far from least, she slid her citrine on the middle finger of her right hand, feeling its familiar, warm buzz flare momentarily against her skin. "You can do this," she whispered to herself.

She noticed her discarded script pages from the day's scenes, and the promise of a real distraction occurred to her. In her rush to answer her phone call, she hadn't realized that her next film's script had yet to be delivered. Given her anticipation over it, she should *definitely* go directly to the production offices and see if she could pick it up, rather than wait.

Lina fought the urge to roll her eyes at herself. Not that it stopped her from walking straight out the door. She'd only gone a few steps and rounded a corner when she slammed headlong into a compact, sturdy chest.

"Oof!"

She looked up into a pair of wide brown eyes, set in what was probably a handsome face, if she could view it from an angle that wasn't obscenely close and therefore a bit fuzzy. She registered the man's gingery hair and his slightly stunned expression, at the same moment a tingle of sparks lit her from within—as it had with her ring, only on a much larger scale.

Still tangled up with him, she blinked in confusion. Her magic had been largely dormant for years. Why it should respond to this *human* stranger, she had no idea.

But then she noticed it: a series of high-pitched mewls, some plaintive and others mischievous. The sound snapped them both into action, and as they attempted to disentangle themselves, Lina realized that they were inundated with … *kittens*?

Well, that explains it. An odd sting of disappointment followed.

A belated air of alarm wafted off the handsome, ginger wall of a gent. "Fucking hell!" He immediately caught himself, his cheeks flooding with color. "Sorry," he mumbled with a frantic glance around them.

Lina attempted to catch her breath as she took in the scene. The man sprang into motion and righted a large basket that had fallen to the ground at their feet, placing the nearest two kittens in it straightaway, all while reaching for a third. He was surprisingly agile, with an almost feline grace of his own.

If the kittens weren't so damn adorable and distracting, she could have watched him move all day.

Her newly reawakened magic pulsed again, strongest near her midsection, where Lina finally noticed the brown-and-white kitty clinging to her waist. She got to work disengaging its tiny claws from her belt. No easy task, either—he was a strong wee fella.

"I don't believe this," her fellow wrangler muttered testily as the previously contained kittens attempted another jail-break. He admonished one, calling it a name that sounded something like "Parm."

As he laid a firm but gentle hand on the little guy's back, Lina was struck by his kindness with the kittens. Despite their current efforts, they clearly adored and trusted him.

Her magic gave its strongest flare yet, and she fought to contain a visible shiver. Sensing it anyway, the third kitten he'd scooped up, a precious gray lass, squirmed in his grasp and reached a paw in Lina's direction.

The man swiftly bent to put her in the basket with the others, all while warding off further escape attempts. "Oh no, you don't. Just because this lady gave you the chance to break out, it doesn't mean she's your new best friend."

"Hey! You ran into me," Lina protested.

He straightened and attempted to scowl at her. He would have been far more likely to succeed were it not for the brindled fuzzball newly attempting to crawl beneath the neck of his sweater. She nearly snickered in his face.

He didn't notice, instead growling, "Because *you* weren't looking where you were going!"

Her humor vanished, and she let out an indignant sound. "Neither were you," she retorted.

He made a largely incoherent grumble, something about "needing" and "job," then managed to transfer his furry ascot to the basket before crouching down to snag another escapee, seconds before it disappeared underneath a nearby crate.

Just how many kittens were in there, anyway?

Unlike the cats, the energy sparking beneath her skin had subsided to a quieter, more controlled buzz. Now that she could finally look at her stranger with some perspective, she confirmed her earlier suspicion—he was indeed handsome, in a rugged sort of way. His nose appeared to have been broken at one time, and he'd clearly missed a couple of spots near his jaw when shaving. All in all, he was a little unpolished, but it worked in his favor.

Too bad he was a bit of a grouch.

Lest he catch her looking, Lina refocused on her little belt-clinger, finally getting him loose. She bent to add him to the container, only to have the rest of the kittens nearly topple the basket over in their efforts to lavish her with attention. *Whoops.* And there went her power, sparking anew. Probably not a bad idea to get out of here soon, since the magic suddenly seemed to have a mind of its own.

Stepping back, she barely managed to dodge a last-minute swipe at her leg. "Not the pantyhose, my good sir," she crooned with a chuckle.

Mr. Sourpuss let out a snort at that, though whether he was laughing at the cat, or her, or simply battling indigestion, she couldn't tell. Her little buddy chose that moment to refocus on his minder, both front paws reaching out to latch onto the man's pant leg.

He let out a long-suffering sigh. "Muenster, no."

Lina couldn't contain her amused huff at the cheesy name. But the gimlet stare he leveled at her stopped any ensuing quippy comments in their tracks.

"Here, let me help you," she offered instead.

They reached for the kitten simultaneously, and an electric jolt

—more than just her magic—shot through her when their fingers brushed. *Good goddess.*

He snatched his hand back as if she'd bitten him, which stung far more than it should have. Alone in her task now, she managed to pluck the cat from his trousers.

Right as he snapped, "Haven't you done enough already? Please, just leave us alone."

Chapter Two

Tony Benson regretted his words the minute they left his mouth.

He'd just lost his cool and yelled at a movie star. Probably not the best course of action for someone trying to turn his current gig as an animal trainer into long-term work at her studio.

But in his defense, Lina Leonard, the seductive queen of some of his favorite noir films, had nearly knocked him on his ass—figuratively and literally. He'd always thought she was a knockout, like a brunette Lauren Bacall with an even huskier, sultrier voice. But seeing her up close, up *very* close...

Tony realized with a start that he'd never, before today, seen the woman in color. All her films were black-and-white. The cameras had never picked up that she had the most delightful spray of faint freckles across her nose and cheekbones. The eyes he'd assumed to be blue were, in fact, an almost golden hazel.

And they currently flashed angrily at him.

Dammit. Guilt zinged through him. True, she'd scattered his cats everywhere. And yes, the slightest touch of her skin against his had set off a volume of fireworks that was downright alarming ... and ... Anyway. He'd been rude, unforgivably so.

But before he could begin to correct his mistake, she spoke.

"Fine." She returned Muenster to his previous spot on Tony's pants before straightening to her full height, looking for all the world like she was tempted to take a bite out of him. And not the good kind.

Lina stepped around the basket and another of the escapees. While he made a grab for the wayward cat, she sent her best femme fatale glare over her shoulder. "Enjoy wrangling your bloody kittens yourself."

Tony croaked a feeble protest as she stalked away. Even Betty —the (mostly) domesticated leopard he'd taken in at the sanctuary he ran when not on a movie set—had never looked as fierce as the woman he'd just offended.

Thankfully, thoughts of Betty reminded him precisely why he needed this job so badly, which pulled him from any descent into woolgathering. A run-in with a film star would be far less detrimental to his job than the failure to get these kittens under control.

He deposited Muenster gently back in the basket, and thankfully the others he'd managed to herd were distracted enough by their brother not to attempt another escape. He noticed, just in time, that tiny Brie had started to trot after Lina, and snagged her before she could get too far.

He raked his fingers through his hair. His day had been going so well; the kittens aced their first morning of filming. And then … all hell broke loose, thanks to Lina. Her presence sure had riled up the kittens.

Not only the kittens.

He bit back a groan, as his earlier anger and anxiety—and attraction—returned. Fine, if he was being honest, he was the one being railed. *Riled!* Geez, she'd made Swiss cheese of his brain. Perhaps she'd zapped him with actual electricity when her hand brushed his.

But none of that mattered now. He needed to focus. If he didn't get his kittens rounded up, he'd never get them through the rest of this movie. And if he didn't get through this movie, he'd never secure more work at the studio. Which would, in turn, attract the funding he needed to keep his animal sanctuary going. So he could help Betty, not to mention Rupert and the horses, and that additional new leopard they'd taken in temporarily…

Breathe. You can do this. One step at a time. Kittens first.

Tony bent over the basket for a head count. "One, two, three, four, five, six…" *Shit.* He examined the cats more closely. "Where the hell is Gouda?"

He should've known. The litter would scramble when provoked, but Gouda rarely needed encouragement to pull a vanishing act. For one so tiny, she was his biggest troublemaker.

Panic clawed up his chest more acutely than any cat's paws. Scrappy as she might be, Gouda was still just a kitten. Wandering among huge equipment and rushing people. Not to mention that huge water tank in the north corner of the property. Tony shuddered. "Oh, god, she could be anywhere," he muttered.

He whipped his head around, frantic to find her. Luckily, he spied a streak of gray fluff disappearing through the doorway of Soundstage Three, where they'd been filming before their break. Relief flooded him.

Tony swept up the kittens' basket and made a beeline for the doorway. After the bright sunshine outside, it took his eyes a minute to adjust to the much darker stage. Once they did, his stomach plummeted all over again.

The reason he'd taken his charges outside in the first place was so the crew could readjust the set and equipment for a new scene —and they were far from finished. The cavernous room was a giant bustle of activity. Crew in motion. Hulking equipment. Endless corners and shadows for a kitten to get lost. And hurt.

He swallowed the panicked whimper that threatened to escape his throat. *Calm. Stay calm. Gouda's smart, you trained her well, you can find her now.*

His sharp inhale brought with it the scent of fresh lumber, which, rather surprisingly, grounded him. He could do this.

But first, he needed to secure Gouda's siblings in their designated pen in the corner. It was only a large child's playpen that someone had rustled up from the bowels of the prop department, but Tony had lined it with blankets, treats, and toys. Most importantly, it was a safe space to keep the cats occupied and comfortable between takes—and nearly impossible for them to break out of.

A lighting grip gave him a friendly wave, and Tony returned it with an approximation of a smile. While it might be helpful to enlist others in his search, he feared the repercussions. If he found Gouda, with no one else the wiser, he'd be far less likely to lose his job. And his means of protecting them all.

Plus, Gouda had already developed a talent for vanishing even more thoroughly once she knew people were searching for her. She'd singlehandedly turn his hair gray before he hit thirty-five.

"Oh good, you're back!" A camera technician grinned in passing.

Tony swallowed. "Are you ready to begin filming again?"

"Not yet. But you wouldn't believe how many people have stopped by, from all over the lot, wanting to play with those guys." He gestured at the kittens and chuckled as he continued on his way.

Tony let out a weak laugh of his own, then scanned the room as intensively, and surreptitiously, as he could. Just when he was ready to give up hope… *There.*

An unused room of the apartment set contained a pair of heavy curtains—and a gray ball of fluff that did not match them. "Oh no," he said under his breath. He noticed the curtains' border of tasseled trim at precisely the same moment Gouda did. One tiny paw reached up to bat them. He had to get to her before she made a mess of the art director's work.

"Tony, hello!"

Shit.

He turned at the greeting to see a cheerful Nick Bradley ambling toward him. In addition to being a talented actor and comedy producer, the man was married to the head of the whole studio. Tony's boss in more ways than one. The very last person he needed to see at the moment.

He gulped. "Hello, Mr. Bradley."

Nick scoffed. "Please. It's Nick." He rubbed his hands together. "How's it going? I heard the cats were a huge hit this morning, so I came by to see for myself." He glanced at the pen behind Tony, and his eyes lit up. "Aw, they're even cuter in person!"

Despite Tony's looming terror, he focused on Nick's infectious enthusiasm. Better to keep him talking so he wouldn't notice the stray kitty clawing at the drapes. "Cat person, are you?"

"I didn't think I was, till I met my wife's." He grinned. "Now I'm hooked."

They shared a chuckle. With Nick's attention on the kittens, Tony risked a glance in Gouda's direction … only to find her gone again.

Fuck me.

He'd be impressed with her stealth, if it wasn't so detrimental to his anxiety levels.

His eyes fell on a costume rack being wheeled across the set, and he squinted at it. Funny, it looked like the coat on the end had one plain sleeve and one fur-trimmed. It must still be a work in prog— *Ohhhh shit.*

"Say, I've been meaning to talk to you." Nick's voice pulled Tony away from his horrific realization.

"Oh?" Tony willed his voice calm.

"We have a comedy coming up on the docket soon. It's a fun script, a bit of a send-up of *Cat People* … with a hefty dash of *Arsenic and Old Lace.*"

A snort of amusement slipped past Tony's inner panic. "That's intriguing."

"It revolves around a single woman who keeps a retired, tame circus cat as a pet. All is well until a string of bad luck starts to befall her uninspiring dates." Nick smirked. "And instead of little old ladies doing mercy killings … the cat's the prime suspect."

Tony's eyebrows flew up.

Nick raised a hand. "But rest assured, the cat won't be a villain. Colin, our screenwriter, is coming up with a few options for the ending, depending on what the censors—and audiences—will let us get away with."

"That sounds rather fantastic, actually."

"Doesn't it? Which brings me to my point. Got a bigger cat we can upgrade to?"

Tony inhaled. Here it was, exactly what he'd hoped for. And he could easily blow it all, if he didn't retrieve Gouda…

Nick continued, "You work with less domestic animals at your sanctuary, right?"

"I do," Tony replied.

"We're still hammering out the details, but we'll need something … wild. Circus-y. Like a panther. Or even a mountain lion could work? Anything like that up your sleeve, with a few tricks up its sleeve?"

Tony's heart raced with excitement, at precisely the moment the wardrobe assistant reached their side of the stage. He tried to keep his eyes on Nick, but as the costumes whizzed behind him, he risked a glance at the coat … which now lacked any fur, anywhere.

He bit back a groan, and instead blurted, "I have a leopard." *Did that sound too desperate?*

Nick rubbed his chin absently. "Hmm. Maybe."

Tony didn't have time to be disappointed, because as he ran a hand through his hair, his peripheral vision took in the rafters above them. And the kitten zipping blithely across a beam.

Oh, for the love of… Honestly, how the fuck…?

Blessedly misinterpreting the look on Tony's face as the mere disappointment he longed to feel, Nick rushed on. "Not that I doubt you. It's just, we talked about one earlier, but I wasn't sure, what with that other film a while back, the one with Grant and Hepburn—and the leopard." He leaned in with a grimace. "I loved it, but it didn't do so well. Might be better to avoid comparisons."

"Oh, right," he managed. "That makes sense." *Try not to panic. Or let Nick look up.*

Nick brightened, oblivious to any impending tumult. "But maybe it's been enough years, and we can pull it off if we do it right. Let's at least give your leopard... Does he or she have a name?"

He willed his focus to remain on the conversation. "She. And it's Betty," he filled in.

"Betty. I love it! We can absolutely give Betty an audition and screen test."

Tony exhaled, tentative elation chipping away at his worry. "That would be terrific. Thanks."

He used the excuse of again smoothing his hair to glance up at ... the now-empty rafters. If he believed in reincarnation, he'd know exactly where Houdini ended up.

A kitten-sized part of him wondered if he should come clean with Nick. He'd be shooting himself in the foot, but if Gouda roamed free for much longer, someone was bound to notice her. Or worse, she'd get herself seriously hurt. And he couldn't live with himself if something happened to her.

"Listen, Nick. I—"

"So sorry I'm late!"

Tony whipped around at the husky voice and was immediately startled by a pair of golden orbs, flashing eerily in the dim lighting. He blinked to clear his mind from the tricks it clearly played on him, and found the reality of Lina Leonard, femme fatale extraordinaire, rushing toward them. Backlit as she was against the stage's open doorway, he almost missed what she cradled in her arms, nearly the same color as her sweater. It wasn't until she reached them that Tony spotted a pair of familiar bright blue eyes staring out at him...

Gouda? *Gouda!*

He came close to shouting her name out loud, before remembering Nick's presence. Instead, he stared in stunned silence as Lina's lips, which he'd watched curve seductively on screen, broke into a bright smile that transformed her entire face.

He had absolutely no idea how Gouda had so quickly escaped the soundstage, only to end up in Lina's hands. But between the dizzying magnificence of her smile, and his overwhelming relief, he wanted nothing more than to kiss the woman until his breath ran out. As if that would ever happen, given that she very likely thought him an utter jackass. Guilt for his earlier rudeness flooded him all over again.

She shot him an analytical glance; then, when words continued to fail him, breezed on. "I hope I haven't held anyone up! I completely lost track of the time." She flashed that mega-watt grin at Nick as she gestured at Tony with her free hand. "I just adore cats, and this gent generously let me spend some quality time with this sweetheart." She emphasized her point with a nuzzle against Gouda's furry head.

For her part, the little adventuress cuddled right back with the most contented purr he'd ever heard, as if she hadn't just been engaged in all sorts of mayhem.

"Anyway," Lina continued. "Before I knew it, my break flew by, and I skedaddled right over here."

Skedaddled? The word should have sounded ridiculous in her noir-dame voice, but the fact that she used it earnestly, rather than in mockery like she would in her films, only intrigued him more.

"I don't blame you," Nick replied, clearly in full control of his faculties, the lucky bastard. "These guys and gals are the sole reason I'm crashing the set today."

"They're the cutest." Lina turned deceptively guileless eyes on Tony. "Please tell me I didn't cause any production delays?"

His voice finally returned to him with a croak. "No." He cleared his throat. "Not at all. Everyone's still setting up."

"Oh, that's such a relief," she breathed.

Their eyes locked, and Tony was once again startled by the

golden hue of hers. His confusion mounted—after their previous altercation, he was baffled as to why she'd help him.

Nick didn't give him time to dwell on the matter. "Say, this is fantastic, you two already knowing each other." He paused in scratching Gouda under the chin and raised his eyes to Lina. "Lois told me you're on board to star in my new comedy. I'm so glad. It's going to be great fun."

"I'm looking forward to it," she replied. "As a matter of fact, I just tried to pick up the script, but apparently it's not quite ready yet. But Mr. Canfield said it involves a big jungle cat?"

As Nick launched into the same details he'd shared moments earlier, Tony watched in fascination as Lina's eyes lit up, practically glowing with her excitement.

"And we've got Yvette Aaron lined up to play your character's best friend," Nick added.

Lina beamed, nearly blinding Tony. "The femme fatale and the scream queen teaming up, eh? So you're leaning into the type-casting…?"

"While simultaneously pushing against it and playing it for satirical laughs?" Nick grinned. "That's the aim."

"Well, now I'm even more ready to get started."

"Excellent." Nick gestured in Tony's direction. "Tony and I were just chatting about it. You two might be working together too."

"Oh. Right." Realization hit Tony square in the chest. He'd been so distracted by how stunning Lina was in every way that it took Nick spelling it out for it to hit him. If he landed Betty this job, they'd be working alongside *Lina Leonard*.

The prospect should thrill him to bits—except he'd just made a terrible first impression on her.

"Tony," Lina said under her breath. With a jolt, he remembered that he hadn't even bothered to introduce himself when they'd been herding the kittens. God, what she must think of him.

She gave Gouda a little scratch with her red-manicured index finger, and continued, "So will there be kittens involved, too?"

Nick chimed in before Tony could answer. "Adorable and tempting, but sadly, no. Tony also has a leopard, so we're going to give her a shot." He paused. "Hell, I should've asked this sooner. You'd be comfortable acting with a highly trained but wild animal, right?"

Lina's lips curved knowingly, as if she was enjoying a private joke. "I think I can manage." She turned her attention to Tony. "How about your leopard? Will she be comfortable acting with a highly trained but wild actor?"

A surprised bark of laughter escaped Tony. "I think she'll manage." He sobered slightly, wanting to give Nick a little extra convincing. "All kidding aside, Betty can absolutely handle the role, even though it'll be her first. She might not have a ton of fancy tricks in her arsenal yet, but I've got her well trained. She can hit marks and obey commands. And she's great with people, truly."

"Betty? Cute," Lina murmured.

Tony fought to suppress his blush.

"Sounds promising," Nick answered. "The people part is the most important thing. I'll talk to the rest of the team and see if they like the idea, but we'll at least give her an audition." He rubbed his hands together. "Well, I'll let you get back to it. Tony, give me a call next week and we'll get the ball rolling."

"You bet. Thanks, Nick."

He departed with a cheery wave, leaving Tony and Lina alone, in awkward silence. Gouda broke it with a squeak.

"You found her," Tony stated obviously. He exhaled, and infused his voice with his genuine gratitude. "Thank you."

Lina nodded. "I was on my way back when she came trotting out of the building, right in front of me. I figured she wasn't supposed to do that."

"No. She wasn't." He tried to aim a stern look at Gouda, but he was just so damn relieved to have her back.

Lina fingered the little tag on her collar. "So you're Gouda." She lifted the kitten to eye level. "Goudini, more like."

He laughed. "That's a good one. And alarmingly accurate."

Lina kissed the top of Gouda's head before handing her back to him. Her fingers were searing as they brushed his, and it was all he could do not to jump in surprise at their shared spark.

All too quickly, she withdrew her hand. "I'm glad I found her when I did."

"Me too." He tried to focus on Gouda's warm weight in his hands, not Lina's heated touch. Unsuccessfully. "Why did you help me?" he blurted.

Her eyes widened, but she didn't answer right away.

So he blustered on. "With Nick, I mean. You didn't have to cover for me. But you did. Even though earlier, I was…"

"Cranky?" Those gorgeous lips curved into a smirk.

"I was going to say a right ass, but … yeah, that too."

She watched him for a moment, assessing his face and then taking in the way he held Gouda. "Who said I did it for you, and not her?" Her gorgeous eyes held little malice, despite her teasing. She shrugged elegantly. "Anyway, everyone has a bad day from time to time. Break lots of little legs today." She reached over to give Gouda's head one last scritch.

She'd taken a few steps away when she added over her shoulder, "See you around the leopard pen."

Tony watched her slink away, forgetting to care that his mouth was probably hanging open. Since the moment he ran into her, he'd felt like he'd been clobbered by a two-by-four. Repeatedly. His open mouth split into a grin, as it dawned on him how much more walloping was in his future, if they ended up working together. He very much looked forward to it.

Gouda's velvety head butted him in the jaw, a sign of her affection.

"Yeah, yeah," he muttered to her. "Go join your brothers and sisters, you little miscreant." He paused before lowering her into the pen. "But no more tricks, missy."

Her replying mewl didn't exactly sound like a promise.

Chapter Three

A few evenings later, Tony straightened his tie and glanced around the crowded bar lounge. The room contained an interesting collection of shiny, glamorous types mingling with more casual folks. To his astonishment, they were indeed interacting, with none of the separation between on- and off-screen one might expect at an after-hours Hollywood gathering.

Apparently, Phoenix Pictures often held these mixers, where they'd rent out a venue for an evening of community-fostering. It seemed to be working; an air of relaxed, genuine conviviality hung over the group.

As he headed toward the bar, the atmosphere helped to quiet his nerves over not knowing many people. The kittens had wrapped their picture, and Betty's audition wasn't until the following week, so he'd been pleasantly surprised to receive an invitation to the festivities.

Nick and his wife, Lois Ashford, were at the center of a small group, engrossed in lively conversation, but Tony didn't have nearly enough courage to join them. A quick perusal of the crowd failed to reveal the actress he most wanted to see this evening— though he had a feeling his courage would desert him that much more if she were there. Luckily, he spotted a friendly face halfway across the room.

"Well, if it isn't everyone's favorite cat guy!" Opal Prince grinned at him, arms wide.

Opal headed up the studio's makeup department and was damn good at her job. The two of them had become friends while working on a few projects together over the years, after initially bonding over being fellow redheads—though hers was several shades brassier than his. She'd been the one to get him in the door at Phoenix, as a matter of fact.

Tony chuckled as he leaned in to buss her on the cheek. "I don't know that I'd go that far, but the kittens did pretty well."

"Please. You and your little buddies have been the talk of the studio all week." She leaned in conspiratorially. "And I hear your leopard's up for a starring role?"

"Wow, news travels fast. Or do you just know everything?" he teased.

She winked. "Little bit of both."

"Well, keep your fingers crossed. Betty doesn't have the part yet. I've got to get her through the audition first."

Opal waved a dismissive hand. "You're both going to nail it, don't worry."

"Thanks. Say, where's your hubby?"

Her cheeks took on an extra bit of pink, as they always did when the subject came up. Her husband Adrian was a fairly popular actor, and the two of them were downright adorable together.

"He had a long day of filming today, so he's meeting me here when he's done."

Tony nodded. "Hey, speaking of filming and actors, do you know if Lina Leonard might be here tonight?"

Opal slowly arched an eyebrow. "She's been known to turn up at these events."

His neck heated under her scrutiny. "Don't look at me like that. She's set to be in the picture Betty's up for. And I wanted to

… thank her again. For … something the other day," he finished, rather pathetically.

"Oh, really?"

"Mm-hmm."

Of course she wouldn't let him off the hook that easily. Her other eyebrow joined its raised mate, and she waited until he relented.

"There was a bit of an … incident. Our introduction didn't go terribly well." *It had, in fact, gone … well, terribly.* "But then Miss Leonard did me a solid, when I, um…" He glanced around and finished quietly, "I may have temporarily, and briefly, misplaced one of the kittens."

Opal's eyes widened. "You *lost* a kitten?" At his wince, she lowered her voice and softened her tone. "Sorry. It's just, all that equipment…" She shuddered. "But the cat's okay, right?"

"She is, thank god. I swear this one might have more than nine lives in her." He sighed. "Anyway, it all worked out."

"That's a relief."

"I'll say. I thought for sure I'd have to pack it all in, give up working at the studio *and* the sanctuary. Rehome all the animals. You might've been adopting a cat. Or several."

"You are far too dramatic, you know that?" She shook her head with a fond smile. "I'm sure it wouldn't have come to all that. You'd have found her even without whatever assistance Lina offered." She smirked. "Besides, while I appreciate the vote of confidence that I could be trusted with a feline, I'm really more of a fish gal myself."

"Fair enough."

Opal looked to be on the verge of saying more, and Tony braced himself for a grilling—he knew he'd been less than subtle with regard to Lina. Fortunately for him, someone in the crowd called out to Opal.

"I've got to go say hi. Want to join me?" she asked Tony.

"I think I'll grab a drink first, if you don't mind."

They parted ways amicably, and Tony resumed his earlier

path, feeling a bit lighter. He'd just settled himself on a barstool when a stunning figure near the door caught his attention, and his breath.

Her gold blouse brought out her eyes even at a distance, and her slim black velvet skirt emphasized her every curve. Matching leopard print pumps and a belt completed the picture and made him chuckle. He wasn't sure if Lina Leonard was already dressing for her next part—and hopefully his—or if she simply liked leopards. Either way, she looked perfect.

She waved at someone, but he didn't dare take his eyes off her to find out who. Her focus landed on Tony, and she shot him her sultry smile as she sauntered toward him. He nearly fell off his chair.

"Hello, there," she said, in an almost shy tone that warred with her smile. *What in the world does* she *have to be shy about?*

"Good evening," he croaked out.

"You know, we skipped over the formal introductions when we first met … and again with Nick and Gouda. It's Tony, right? Tony…?"

He tried to control the flush creeping up his neck. "Right. Yes. I'm Tony. Tony Benson. And you're Lina Leonard."

"That's me." She extended her hand. "It's nice to officially meet you, Tony Benson."

"Likewise," he replied, accepting her handshake. Her fingers curved around his, and her palm felt like silky perfection. He swallowed, hard. It was as if she'd transferred the chaos of their first meeting directly into his bloodstream.

She let go first, not that it broke the spell. He watched in fascination as her eyes assessed him, then registered a decision made. "So, Tony. Can I buy you a drink?"

He couldn't contain his surprise.

When he didn't immediately respond, she narrowed her eyes and retorted, "Unless you're one of those fellas who can't abide a gal doing the buying?"

Thankfully, he found his voice. "No! Of course not. I'm just a bit startled you'd want to."

"You mean after that stellar first impression you made?" Her eyes twinkled with mischief.

He chuckled ruefully. "Exactly."

"It did work out all right in the end."

"Thanks largely to you." He swallowed. "I want to thank you, again. And to apologize, also again. You caught me at a stressful moment, but that's no excuse. Believe me, I'm not in the habit of yelling at movie stars."

Lina raised her eyebrows. "Ah, so that's it, is it? You're only sorry because I'm a movie star?"

Her tone was playful, teasing, but underneath it Tony detected something else. Something like disappointment. He found himself wanting to reassure her with more honesty.

"I'll admit, I did worry about that, at first. But no. My apology, now, has everything to do with correcting the rocky start I got off to with a rather charming lady … despite how many of her films I may or may not have seen." Her smile softened, and it emboldened him. "So, how about we buy each other a drink?"

"Deal."

Lina perched on the stool next to him, and he caught a whiff of her perfume, the scent somehow soft and spicy at the same time. Full of contradictions, like her. She waved the bartender over.

"Evening, Miss Leonard." The older, round-cheeked man gave her a jovial nod. "What can I get you?"

"Hi, Oscar. I'd love a martini, extra olives. Thanks."

Oscar turned expectantly to Tony. "I'll also have a martini. But *no* olives. Thank you."

"Coming right up, folks." Oscar left them to fix their drinks.

Lina shot Tony an incredulous look. "No olives? Really? Is that even still a martini?"

He shrugged. "Just not my cup of tea."

"Oh, well, that explains it. You've been using them all wrong."

She leaned in and stage-whispered, "Olives taste *terrible* in tea, you know."

Hearty laughter rumbled from his chest. "I'll take that under advisement, thanks."

They grinned at each other until Oscar returned with their drinks. Lina immediately plucked the olive-laden toothpick out of her glass and slid one off with her teeth. In an effort to keep all his blood from rushing south, Tony raised his glass.

"To second, less feline, impressions," he toasted.

Lina's lips curved into a smile. "I don't know, I liked the cats. How about… To getting off on a better foot … or paw?" At his laugh, she let out a husky chuckle of her own. "Either way, cheers."

"Cheers."

They clinked glassware and each took a sip. Warmth settled in Tony's chest that had nothing to do with the smooth cocktail.

Lina glanced down at her drink, then his. "Hmm. How does the whole buying each other drinks thing work, when we ordered the same?"

He paused dramatically, considering. "Bit of a *catch*-22, I guess."

Lina snorted. "Not bad."

"Thanks." Tony grinned. "And I honestly have no idea about the drinks, but I'm not too worried about the semantics. It's the thought that counts."

Lina agreed with another tap of her cocktail against his. They sipped their drinks in companionable silence for a few moments, before Tony's curiosity won out. He gestured to her shoes. "Fan of leopard print, are you?"

At precisely the same moment, Lina asked, "So, how'd you come to have a leopard?"

They laughed together.

He extended a hand in her direction. "Please, ladies first."

"Well, in answer to *your* question, yes. I do love the print." Tony sensed a story there, but she didn't let him probe further.

"Which is why I'm so curious about your vast cornucopia of cats." She leaned an elbow on the bar and rested her chin in her hand. "Tell me about this Betty of yours."

His menagerie was a favorite unprompted topic of conversation, so to have someone actually ask him about it? Tony beamed.

"Betty's my pride and joy. I've had her since she was a tiny cub." He grimaced at the memory of the day she'd come into his life. "A few years ago—not too long after the war, actually—I was driving past the site of a circus that had just left town, and something caught my eye by the side of the road. I spotted her tiny spots first. I pulled over, and there she was. Abandoned, hungry. One of her paws hurt."

Lina let out an incensed huff, and her anger on Betty's behalf gratified him.

"It took a few minutes for the red haze to clear my vision," he continued. "But then I scooped her up, took her home, nursed her back to health…"

"And you've been together ever since?" Lina smiled warmly, now that they'd gotten to the happier part of Betty's story.

"Yep." His chest swelled with pride. "She's the sweetest thing. You're going to love her." He hoped he wasn't gushing too much, but if anything, Lina's expression seemed to have melted further. "And for the record, it isn't only cats I'm responsible for. When I'm not on a movie set, my cousin Carl and I run a shelter of sorts, up in the hills. At the moment, we have Betty and the kittens, plus a monkey and even a couple of horses."

Lina's eyes widened. "Wait, not the Applegate Sanctuary?"

"That's ours, yeah. You've actually heard of it?"

She nodded. "My friend told me about it. She works in … conservation and … rescues, I guess you'd say. Anyway, she keeps up with organizations like yours. According to her, you're providing a great service. Anyone helping to foster and rehabilitate animals is aces in her book—and mine—but the way you balance the performing element, in a way that actually takes into account what *they* need…" She cleared her throat, seeming to catch herself having gotten carried away. "It's admirable."

Tony blinked, gobsmacked at both her enthusiasm for his work and the fact that she knew so much about it in the first place. "Wow. Thank you. That's … good to hear."

"You sound surprised."

"Truth be told, I am, a little." He huffed a laugh. "I mean, I believe wholeheartedly in what we do. And if I can inspire more folks in entertainment to work with animals ethically, even better. But all too often lately, it feels like Carl and I are barely keeping our heads above water. It's been our dream forever, and we finally decided to make a go of it after the war. We've been at it for a couple years now, and while we're doing okay…"

"Okay isn't quite good enough?" Lina asked gently.

"I'm afraid not. I know we can get there, but Carl is restless. He also works at the zoo, as a vet, and they want him full time. Plus he got married last year, and I think it's weighing on him more than he'll admit. I can't blame him. We could be doing so much if we had more resources, plain and simple." He shrugged.

"And let me guess. A steady gig with a Hollywood studio would go a long way toward getting you those resources?"

God, simply being able to unburden himself lifted a tremendous weight off his shoulders. As did her understanding, and her empathy. To think, he'd nearly misjudged this woman.

"I believe it would make a tremendous difference." Tony rubbed his neck and offered her a sheepish smile. "That's why I got so cranky over the kittens the other day. The stakes feel so damn high sometimes."

"I get it."

He met her eyes directly. "I am glad that Gouda crossed your path when she escaped."

"Me too." Her dazzling smile flashed again. "And your kittens may have gotten you in the door, but I have no doubt Betty'll keep you on the inside."

"I hope so. Nick didn't seem too sure about casting a leopard. But she's all I've got."

Lina waved a dismissive hand. "Don't worry about it. You've got him mostly convinced already. And I'll be sure to talk you up. If Betty's half as charming as you say, I'm sure you're a shoo-in."

Her encouragement made him feel ten feet off the ground. "I'll drink to that."

They lifted their glasses in another toast, and Tony had barely swallowed his sip when an idea occurred to him. He voiced it before he lost his nerve.

"Say, would you like to meet Betty? Before her audition, I mean? You could come out to Applegate."

Lina beamed, her hazel eyes taking on a lovely golden cast. "Oh, that sounds marvelous! I would absolutely love to. Can I bring her a treat of some kind? Does she have a sweet tooth to match her personality?"

Tony held in a laugh, instead folding his arms across his chest with mock sternness. "Are you trying to bribe my cat, Miss Leonard?"

Her expression turned saucy. "Of course."

"I should warn you, it'll cost you." He leaned in conspiratorially. "She's partial to filet mignon."

"Expensive taste. A gal after my own heart." She winked.

The pair of them settled into their barstools, the conversation —and laughter—flowing easily between them. Tony lost all track of how long they sat there. At one point, he spied Opal watching him with barely concealed glee; he was dimly aware he should attempt to ward her off, or at least go and greet the finally-arrived Adrian—but remained rooted to his spot opposite Lina.

She fascinated him more with each passing minute. Talking to her, he easily forgot she was a movie star, one of the most gorgeous people he'd ever encountered, someone who should be far above an ordinary guy like him. Her warmth, her friendly nature, those endlessly charming freckles, pulled him in like a magnet.

Even so, when the party started winding down and Tony walked Lina out, he half expected to put her into a car with a hired driver. He shouldn't have been surprised when she led him to the parking lot, and her sleek Oldsmobile coupe, instead.

"I had a lovely time this evening, Mr. Benson," she purred, her playful tone belying her formal words.

"As did I, Miss Leonard." Following her lead, he executed a small bow. Her resulting husky chuckle hit him right below the belt.

"So Tuesday's good, to come out to the sanctuary?"

"Yes. Mornings are usually a little busy, what with everyone's feedings and my morning check-ins, but feel free to stop by anytime in the afternoon. I can't wait to introduce you to Betty."

"I can't wait to meet her." Her eyes glowed under the soft light of the streetlamps.

Tony glanced around the quiet lot. A few cars remained, but the area was empty of people, save for them. Feeling bold, he leaned down to brush a kiss across her soft cheek. The audible hitch of her breath gratified him. "Thanks again for the drink."

"Right back at ya," she whispered, before seeing his boldness and raising him one. Or several.

Her lips met his, featherlight and utterly electrifying. The kiss lasted only a brief moment, but managed to sear him from his head to his toes.

"Good night, Tony."

Before he could catch his breath, she slid into her car. The gentlemanly instincts his mother had instilled in him kicked in on autopilot, in spite of his befuddled head, and he closed the door behind her.

He watched her car as she pulled out of the driveway, and continued to stare, grinning like a fool, long after her taillights vanished into the night.

Chapter Four

*L*ina popped a ginger candy in her mouth as she navigated her coupe along the winding road that led to Applegate Sanctuary. Her nerves fluttered a bit over the prospect of meeting her leopard compatriot in the flesh, especially since her magic had started re-manifesting itself in strange bursts lately. But she was mostly curious about the cat, and excited to see the sanctuary's setup.

And its owner. *Tony…*

She'd been unable to resist kissing him. It had been the briefest of touches, yet it had replayed on a loop in her mind—hell, her entire body—ever since. All the lovely, long while they'd remained at the bar, she only had the one martini, but her buzz had continued to intensify. She'd gotten steadily more fizzy over Tony Benson.

Once he let his guard down, he was rather charming. And funny. His regard for the animals under his care was downright intoxicating. It called to that magical part of her, deep down. No matter that she rarely used it—he made it sing.

Made her want to do a hell of a lot more than just kiss him.

Lina's teeth smashed the candy in her mouth to bits. They

were about to start working together, and this attraction could easily become a distraction. *Or it could make for one hell of a fun film shoot…*

The appearance of Applegate's entrance through the trees on her right brought her back to the present. The short driveway emptied into a clearing with several modest buildings. A ranch house sprawled on one side, with a simple, decent-sized barn in the center. A pair of horses munched on some grass inside a fenced-in pasture. She saw the fence of another enclosure behind it, stretching around the back of the barn, and suspected that was Betty's home.

Lina pulled her car to a stop in the open space in front of the house and got out, and as her shoes crunched on the dirt, she was glad she'd had the sense to wear a pair of flat oxfords today. She inhaled a deep lungful of fresh air and smiled. She didn't know if it was the buildings or the trees surrounding the area, or both, but the woody scent reminded her of pencils. With—she wrinkled her nose—an undercurrent of horse manure.

She grabbed the parcel she'd brought and headed for the barn. Reaching the open door, she spotted Tony inside. He hefted a large sack and began pouring feed of some kind into several smaller containers. His collared shirt stretched nicely over his broad shoulders, and his sleeves were rolled up past his elbows, showing off the corded muscles in his arms as they flexed under the weight of his task.

A rumbling purr started in her chest.

An *audible* rumbling purr. At precisely the moment Tony paused his activity. *Shit.*

His head whipped around, but the moment his face split into a brilliant grin, Lina forgot her embarrassment. Still, she valiantly held in another purr as she watched him set the feed bag down and amble toward her.

"Lina! Hello!"

"Hi. I hope this is an okay time?"

"Of course." He gestured behind him. "I had a few minutes, so I was just getting a jump on dinner prep."

"Speaking of which." She held out her package. "Filet mignon for Betty, as promised."

Tony laughed as he carefully took it from her. "You didn't really need to."

"I wanted to. From all you've told me, the gal deserves a treat."

"Can't argue with that," he said softly.

They stood for a moment in a silence that was somehow awkward and comfortable at the same time. As Lina debated mentioning their kiss, Tony's eyes roved over her face, lingering on her nose again as he had the other night—*could my nose truly be that interesting?*—before settling on her lips.

Maybe I should skip talking and jump right into kissing him again.

A loud screeching to her right broke the quiet instead, and they both jumped as if burned.

"Rupert!" Tony admonished. He pointed to a medium-sized brown monkey hopping around in a large cage. "That's Rupert."

"Hello, Rupert," Lina called.

Tony smiled. "He's typically an affectionate gentleman, but under the circumstances, he gets antsy whenever anyone is here. I think he feels left out." He shrugged. "He got a rock stuck in his foot last week, and he needs to stay contained and away from danger until it's healed a little more."

"Poor thing." She stepped closer to Rupert's cage. "Don't worry, sir. I'm sure you'll be able to join the party in no time."

"That's what I keep telling him, but he doesn't seem to believe me."

Lina flashed a smile over her shoulder at him, then took in the space for the first time. She turned in a slow circle. "Quite an impressive setup you've got here."

Tony's cheeks flushed a delightful shade of pink. "Thanks. We're lucky, the property's been in our family for ages. When Grandpa decided to retire from ranch life, he 'sold' the place to me and Carl for a dollar. Let me give you the full tour." He led her to the center of the room, gesturing around them, his voice taking on a hint of professional formality—and pride. "We converted the stables for treatment and recovery for smaller animals. Carl is the vet, so he did most of the design and setup."

Lina nodded as he guided her to the back of the building, and out into a similar space under a portico.

"We have bigger treatment pens out here. Eventually, we're hoping to expand, create even more out back, where I can focus on physical rehabilitation for the ones who need it." He ran a hand through his thick red waves. "But that's a ways off yet."

"You'll get there." She nodded at the space. "This is really fantastic, Tony."

His throat worked before he spoke. "Thanks." The moment hovered between them; then he shook his head. "Anyway, I'm sure you're ready for the main event." He swept his hand, and she followed him out from under the shelter.

"Oh, wow," she breathed.

The enclosure next to the horses' pasture did indeed span around behind the barn, larger than she'd anticipated. The fence stretched far enough that she couldn't even see its back border. Trees dotted the enclosure, and a cluster of rocks formed an insular, homey cave.

Lounging on top of the cave, tail swishing gently, was the most gorgeous leopard Lina had ever seen, soaking up the sunshine. Granted, she was the *only* leopard Lina had seen this close—she'd abandoned her magical studies early, and thought it best to keep her distance ever since—but that didn't make Betty any less gorgeous.

Her magic clearly agreed. She suppressed a shiver at its sudden presence and snuck a glance at Tony, worried it was somehow visible. Luckily, his attention remained on their surroundings.

Lina ventured closer, then noticed that one corner of the yard was separated from the rest by a locked gate, inside of which reposed…

"You have *two* leopards?"

Tony chuckled beside her. "At the moment, we do, actually." He led her closer but maintained a bit of distance, even though the sleeping cat was unaware of their presence. "That there is Bob. He's staying with us for a bit while he recovers."

"Recovers?"

A muscle twitched in Tony's jaw. "Yeah. Carl got a call about an accident at a circus down in the Valley, and I convinced him to bring Bob here instead of the zoo."

The hairs on the back of Lina's neck bristled, and she raised an eyebrow, her tone matching Tony's. "An accident, huh?"

He pulled a skeptical face. "So they say. I don't trust them as far as I can throw them, but Carl went in person to pick Bob up, and saw nothing outwardly suspect going on. But we're keeping an eye on them."

"Good."

The corners of his mouth tipped up at her conviction, before he sobered again. "On the one hand, it's excellent that his injury is only minor, and he's healing quickly."

"But that means he'll be ready to leave sooner, doesn't it?"

He nodded grimly. "It does. And the jackasses who run the show have already called a few times. He's apparently their star attraction, and they want him back. Carl talked them down, but they're impatient." He sighed. "I wish we could find a way to keep him."

"Me too." This had to be the circus Alice had mentioned. Goddess knew, Lina was hardly qualified to step in for anything but an emergency, but instinct told her it might be necessary to look into them anyway.

"It's good you were able to bring him here, at least for a while," she added.

"I have to admit, it wasn't entirely unselfish. The more we build our reputation, the more goodwill we can raise. But I also suspected it might do wonders for Bob to spend some time with a friendly face." He brightened. "On that note!"

As if on cue, Betty leapt down and padded over to them, and Lina's heart melted, even as her magic flared in a heady sizzle beneath her skin.

"C'mon over."

They approached the fence, but Tony stopped a few feet away. "Be careful to start. I wasn't exaggerating, she's a gentle sweetheart, and I've got her well trained. But she is still a wild animal."

"Understood." While he had no idea what little danger Lina was in, she admired his cautious attitude.

He approached first, extending his hand between the fence bars to gently scratch Betty's head. The leopard responded with an affectionate nuzzle. "There's my good girl."

Bloody hell. One sentence, and she could tell how excellent he was with Betty. One sentence, and Lina's pulse throbbed, right between her legs. She blinked hard, forcing her focus on the leopard and not her minder.

"Betty," he continued, oblivious to Lina's inner turmoil. "There's someone I'd like you to meet. This pretty lady is Lina."

Stop intensifying that turmoil, sir. She bit her lip in an attempt to rein in her lascivious musings.

"You might be spending a lot of time with her, if everything goes according to plan." Tony turned his luminous gaze to Lina. "Lina, this special gal is Betty."

Betty's attention followed his prompting, her expression almost humanly curious. Her pale amber eyes were positively captivating, finally pulling Lina's thoughts firmly away from her libido. She took a slow breath and reached cautiously for her magic, projecting a sense of ease, of trust, to the big cat.

Hot damn, it's working. Betty eased out from under Tony's hand and angled toward Lina.

"Hello, Betty. It's very nice to meet you." Tentatively, she extended her hand toward the fence. Betty met her partway, nudging playfully against her palm, her velvety coat soft under Lina's fingers.

"Atta girl," Tony whispered.

Lina slowly, gently massaged her fingers along the leopard's scalp, delighting when Betty let out a contented rumble. "The rumors were true. You are a sweet lass, aren't you?"

"She rarely lets people get that close so fast. She likes you."

Lina looked up into Tony's beaming face and nearly swooned. "Well." She forced her attention back to Betty. "The feeling is mutual. She's just lovely."

As if on cue, Betty slid to the ground and rolled over, butting her head against Lina's hand. Lina laughed.

"My word, she really is like a giant housecat, isn't she?"

"She certainly has me fooled sometimes," Tony replied, chuckling with her. "Wanna see her do a few tricks?"

Lina cocked an eyebrow. "I thought you told Nick she couldn't do much?"

His cheeks flushed a delightful shade of pink. "I mean, technically … no. She won't jump through a flaming hoop or anything. But we can manage a little basic fetch, can't we, girl?" He reached through the bars to pet Betty's flank, then held a hand up to Lina. "Hold on."

Lina watched with amusement as he ran back to the stables and reemerged with a small bucket.

He unlocked a gate she hadn't even noticed, and glanced over to her apologetically. "I know you're getting along swimmingly, but best if you stay out here for now, if you don't mind."

"Of course."

Tony gave her a decisive nod and stepped through the gate. At his slow approach, Betty got to her feet and padded a few steps toward him, simultaneously eager and gentle. Her affection for Tony wafted off her in waves so palpable, Lina suspected she'd be able to feel them even without her powers.

At this rate, she'd end up in such a puddle Tony might need to escort her off the property in that bucket.

"Hi, sweetheart," he crooned to the leopard. "Want to show off a little for Lina?"

Betty rubbed herself against his leg in response. Tony stepped back and pulled a short, knotted piece of rope from the ground at their feet.

"Okay, Betty." His voice took on a commanding tone that immediately stilled the leopard—and sent an electric chill up Lina's spine. "Are you ready?" He held the rope in front of Betty, letting her focus on it for a moment, before raising it above his head and tossing it past the rocks behind her. "Go find it, girl."

Lina bit her lip, arching her back against a full-body shiver. Betty took off in the direction of the toy, all sleek grace. The cat zipped back around the cluster of rocks, the rope between her teeth, and came to a smooth stop in front of Tony. She dropped her quarry at his feet and promptly sat on her haunches. Tony smiled and reached into the bucket for what looked—and smelled —to be a piece of meat.

"Good girl," he crooned, tossing the meat to her. She caught it easily and bent to gnaw at it.

Lina applauded softly. "Well done!" She glanced up at Tony. "Both of you."

His grin nearly blinded her. "She's gotten really good at that one."

"What else have you got?"

"Well…" He glanced down at Betty, worrying at his lower lip. His very full, very kissable, lower lip. "We have been working on a new trick, but we haven't practiced it much."

Betty finished chewing her treat and looked up at him expectantly. The two of them made an adorable picture.

"So what are you waiting for?" Lina prodded. At his hesitant look, she added, "Even if it's a bit rough around the edges, I'm still going to find it impressive."

His lips curved upward, and he nodded. "All right, then." He scratched the crown of Betty's head. "What do you say we try the new one, huh, Betty? Wanna stand up?"

"Intriguing," Lina said.

Tony flashed her a wink as Betty got to her feet. He reached for another bit of meat, holding it aloft as he had the rope. That firm, deep tone returned to his voice.

"Okay, Betty. Up." He gave a slight flick of his wrist. "Up. That's it."

Lina watched in fascination as Betty rose up, her front paws leaving the ground momentarily. After a couple of false starts, at Tony's continued encouragement, she rose up almost fully on her hind legs, pawing in the direction of his raised arm.

"Good girl," he called, tossing the meat into her waiting mouth.

Betty dropped to the ground, munching happily as she rolled onto her back. Tony leaned down to rub her belly, before turning his sunshine on Lina again.

"That was wonderful!" She reached through the fence to join in on the belly rubs, but her hand froze when a bit of her own sunshine—a literal spark of magic—glowed against Betty's sleek coat. She closed her fist and slowly removed her hand, praying Tony wouldn't notice. When he didn't seem to, she added, "You're very talented, Betty."

Tony's chuckle warmed her to her core and flooded her with relief. *So far, so good.*

"She sure is," he replied. "My goal is to get her to take a few steps, but this is a start."

"A strong one."

"Thanks." He picked up his bucket and tossed Betty one more treat, then made his way back to the gate.

Lina was thoroughly enjoying the sight of him descending the steps from the enclosure when a soft, tingling pressure against her leg, followed by a tiny mewl, distracted her. She looked down to find her buddy Gouda staring back with those wide baby-blues of hers.

"Well, hello, old friend." She bent to scoop the kitten up. With an overabundance of caution, she took a few steps away from the fence. Given everything she'd witnessed today, and Gouda's clear lack of hesitation, everything would likely be fine. But the entirety of Gouda was roughly the size of Betty's head, so better safe than sorry.

Tony came to stand in front of them, planting his hands on his hips. "Gouda. Again? You've got to stop this."

"She's not supposed to be this close to Betty, is she?"

Tony shook his head. "No. She's not. And she knows it." He heaved a sigh. "Not that I think Betty's dangerous. As a matter of fact, she seems to find the kittens entertaining. But…" He trailed off, looking over his shoulder at a still-slumbering Bob.

"You don't know how he'll react."

"Right. Not to mention all the coyotes that call this area home."

"Oh, I doubt you'll have trouble from them, not back here at least." At Tony's quizzical look, she lifted her chin in Betty's direction. "You couldn't ask for a better bodyguard."

"So long as the bodyguard can keep her claws to herself."

Lina nodded, and lifted Gouda. "See. You need to be more careful, missy. Listen to Tony, he knows his stuff."

She met his eyes, and they both grinned. He opened his mouth to speak, but was interrupted by the appearance of two more kitties. Lina immediately recognized her belt-clinger from the other day, but she hadn't made the acquaintance of his calico friend yet.

"Aaand she let them all out," Tony muttered. "Swell."

Lina crouched, rubbing her index finger over her pal's head. "I remember you. Muenster, right? And who's this little fella?" She pointed to the third cat.

"That's Parm."

She bit back her smile. So that *was* what she'd heard the other day. "Nice to meet you, Parm." She stood again, in time to catch the rising flush on Tony's neck.

Before she could tease him, they were joined by yet another kitten. And another. They ignited a much gentler twinge of her magic than Betty had, but given the sheer number of them, the sensation was still pretty potent. She ought to stay vigilant, but this bunch tended to be sufficiently chaotic that any errant magic should evade Tony's notice.

Sure enough, he groaned at the cats, and Lina laughed. They were surrounded once again, only this time, neither of them minded. He attempted to pick up a couple, but they wriggled out of his grasp. Luckily, they didn't wander, instead clustering around Lina's legs.

Tony's brown eyes twinkled as he arched an eyebrow at her. "What are you, the Pied Piper of Cats?"

She fought to suppress her blush. "Something like that." In an effort to distract him from how close to the truth he was, she nodded at the crowd around her. "So, do I get to formally meet the rest of these cuties?"

With a nod, Tony adopted an air of mock solemnity. "Of course, madam." He pointed to a gray kitten who was nearly Gouda's twin. "That's Brie." A brindled sibling, whom she recognized from his attempt to crawl into Tony's sweater, was next. "And Swiss."

When he got to the last cat, a handsome tuxedo gent, Lina couldn't help her snicker.

"Let me guess … that one's Kraft?" she teased.

He shot her a haughty look. "No. His name is Roquefort."

"My apologies."

Tony cleared his throat, gesturing to their right, where a seventh kitten, this one with a healthy portion of ginger streaks, trotted toward them. *"That's Kraft."*

Lina widened her eyes. "Not really?"

He blushed in earnest now. "Yes. Really."

Lina's laughter burst out of her. "Oh, that's perfection." She lowered her voice to a conspiratorial rasp. "So does that make you the Big Cheese?"

Tony's resulting explosion of mirth was accompanied by a delightful flush, and they stood, surrounded by kittens and fizziness and warmth. When she caught him watching her with appreciation, and a bit of determination, her heart sped up.

He sucked in a breath. "Lina, if we can extract you from these misfits, would you like to go grab dinner with me?"

Would I ever. She nuzzled Gouda. "What do you think, Gouda? Can you keep your siblings in line while I borrow Tony for a bit?"

The cat meowed, and Lina, with blind optimism, took it as an affirmative. "Excellent." She grinned at Tony. "I'd love to."

Chapter Five

"I'm afraid there's not too much to choose from around here, but there are a couple of decent joints down the hill, if you don't mind coming back for your car afterward?" Tony asked hopefully. He knew it made more sense for them to drive separately, but he was reluctant to lose out on any time with Lina.

The more he spent with her, the more he craved.

Hell, even wrangling the wiliest kittens in existence was easier —and loads more fun—with her on his team.

"Not at all," she replied with a seductive smile. It wouldn't be long before he'd be willing to sell his soul for a glimpse of that smile.

He mentally chided himself. *Take it slow; don't push your luck.* As if he needed an extra nudge from the heavens, the telephone's shrill ring from inside the house pierced the air.

Tony gestured over his shoulder. "I should probably get that, sorry. Hopefully it'll just be a minute." At Lina's nod, he turned and jogged up the porch steps, dashing inside to the hall phone.

"Applegate Sanctuary," he answered. "This is Tony."

"Oh, it's you. Where's the vet guy?"

Tony's stomach sank as he recognized the gruff voice. One of the assholes from the circus. He managed, barely, to keep his tone calm. "I beg your pardon?"

"This is Ralph. From Circus Dirkus." *Circus Jerk-us, more like.* "I wanna know when we're getting our leopard back. So let me talk to the vet guy."

Tony bit back a rude retort, knowing it would only anger this ass further. Inhaling through his nose, he said instead, "*Dr.* Benson isn't here at the moment. But I can tell you, your leopard needs a few more days of recovery."

"Oh, come on. How long could it possibly take? The doc said he wasn't hurt bad. Why should I believe you?"

Tony pinched the bridge of his nose. As he turned to lean against the wall, he spotted Lina hovering in the doorway, her golden eyes full of concern. The sight of her gave him an unexpected boost of calm. And courage.

"And the same 'doc' also told you it would still take time for his injuries to heal. Don't you want him to make a full recovery before you put him back to work?"

Ralph grunted. "I want him back. Period. We're coming for him today."

Panic churned in Tony's gut, and his mind raced to come up with an excuse. "No, wait. You need to wait … for Dr. Benson to sign off on his release before you pick him up. Legally," he tacked on. He was fudging the truth with that last bit, but since it seemed to finally make Ralph pause, he had no regrets.

The man issued another grunt, and Tony rushed to add, "The doctor was planning to give him a full checkup again in a couple of days."

"I don't—" A loud clatter in the background interrupted Ralph, and—without bothering to cover the receiver—he shouted, "Dammit, Joey!"

Tony held the phone away from his ear as even more chaos seemed to erupt over the line.

Ralph returned his attention to their call, voice impatient.

"Fine. Whatever. A few more days. But we need him this weekend."

Too soon. "I—"

"And next time, you better put the doc on. I'm not dealing with *you* again." The line went dead with an ominous click.

Tony held out the receiver, giving it a glare as if Ralph could see him through it. "What the hell was that supposed to mean?" he muttered as he returned the phone to its cradle.

Lina's perfume preceded her approach, bringing with it additional calm. "Is everything all right?" she asked softly.

He shook his head. "One of the circus guys again, asking after Bob." He grimaced. "Demanding, actually."

She arched one perfect eyebrow, eyes flashing angrily. "If he's so important to them, shouldn't they be more concerned about his welfare?"

"You would think." His shoulders sagged. "Every instinct is telling me not to give Bob back to them, but I don't know if we can avoid it. Even if we find a reason, we might have to let him go for a bit first."

Lina's hand rested on his arm, rubbing her thumb soothingly along his skin. "I'm sure you'll work it out. Keep the fuckers from winning."

He let out a choked laugh. "I hope so. Thanks."

She squeezed his arm with an encouraging grin. "Now. You need a distraction. And I believe you promised me dinner."

"That I did." He returned her infectious smile. "Let's go."

They moved toward the door together, but without thinking, Tony slowed his pace. He glanced in the direction of the leopard enclosure, his mind still on that phone call. He'd managed to talk the guy down, but his unease lingered over Ralph's threatening tone.

"Unless..." Lina paused. "You'd rather stay close to home? Just in case."

She so effortlessly read his mood, it made his head spin a little.

A weight immediately lifted off his chest at her offer, but another quickly settled in its place. He *had* promised her a date.

"He said he'd accept a few more days, though I wonder if I should stick around, especially without Carl here." He looked down into her gorgeous face. "But…"

She didn't let him finish, again taking charge. "Have you got any food worth eating here?" Her lips curved up.

Yep. Definitely don't need that soul. Take it, it's yours.

Gratitude and desire slammed through him in equal measure. "I might be able to rustle something up. You sure you don't mind?"

"Absolutely not." She reached up to brush a lock of hair off his forehead, and he nearly swooned. "The animals under your care are lucky to have you, Tony."

He captured her hand and pressed a kiss to the center of her palm, thrilled to feel her pulse thrumming rapidly in her wrist. He was tempted to pull her close—whether to kiss her thoroughly or simply to let her hold him, he wasn't quite sure. Perhaps both.

The gentleman in him prevailed. She was offering him such comfort, and he wanted to keep his promise.

He slowly lowered her hand. "Dinner," he rasped. "Let's see what I've got. Or … if you're not too hungry yet, want to see this place first?" He gestured toward the house, suddenly feeling the need to move, to shake off his remaining nervous energy so he could better focus on making this a nice evening for her.

Lina's eyes lit up at the prospect. "Oh, definitely a tour." She gestured down the hall. "Lead the way."

"As you wish." He waved her forward. "Kitchen. Pretty standard."

"I see that."

He moved them along with a chuckle. "Office." He held up a hand. "Please don't look too closely. It's not pretty."

"Do you know where everything is?"

"Of course," he replied with pride.

"Then that's all that matters." She winked.

"Could you please tell Carl that? He never believes me, but I have yet to lose a single thing."

She placed a hand over her heart. "You have my word."

"Thank you, milady."

Her resulting tinkle of laughter was throaty and so damn sexy, he couldn't stand it.

"Anyway," he stumbled on. "Living room. Not that we keep it particularly lived-in."

"You know, I have to admit, I've never understood the idea of a formal living room. Rather defeats the purpose, doesn't it?"

"Yes! Same here." He frowned at the room. "Sadly, we occasionally have to entertain clients and potential investors, so I can't stick to my own belief system in here."

"It does have a homey air to it, if that makes you feel any better."

"A little bit."

While Tony bent to straighten one of the couch cushions, Lina wandered back to the hall. Only a moment passed before she called out, "Hey, what's up here?"

He found her peering up the staircase at the back of the house. "Oh, um… Nothing you need to worry about."

She tilted her head, and her eyebrow hitched again. "You do realize that's a surefire way to send me straight up the stairs, don't you?"

Tony crossed his arms over his chest, attempting to look stern. "And if I told you it's none of your business?"

"Probably wouldn't stop me."

He valiantly suppressed a chuckle.

Leaning her elbow on the newel post, she glanced up the stairs and then back at him. "Hmm. Have you got another leopard stashed up there? Or…" She gasped. "Tony Benson, is your exwife locked upstairs?"

He did laugh at that. "I assure you, I have never been married. Nor would I do that to a lady."

"Unless, of course, the lady was a leopard."

"Precisely."

Her eyes flashed, there and gone before he could decide whether it was humor or something darker. "I notice you didn't deny having a cat up there…"

"A man's got to maintain some air of mystery." He sighed dramatically. "All right, fine. If you must know, that is where I happen to live."

"I… Oh." She didn't hide her open curiosity when she looked up this time. "I didn't realize this is your home, too. And Carl?"

"No." He might be reading too much into it, but she looked relieved at that. "He and his wife have an apartment closer to the city. Though he didn't live here even before they got married." He shrugged. "Sometimes he needs a place of his own, away from work."

Her smile softened. "And you don't?"

"Nah. I like being out here. Plus, the lack of rent is rather appealing."

"I'll bet."

They hovered there, on the edge of the moment, but it didn't take long for him to notice the way she vibrated with anticipation. He relented with a laugh.

"Go ahead."

"Really? You don't mind?"

"I do not."

And he truly didn't, especially when she let out a delighted hum and charged up the stairs. He followed, just in time to catch another gasp, this one genuine, which sent warmth blooming in his chest.

LINA STOPPED short at the top of the stairs, taking in Tony's home. For it was assuredly a home—much more lived-in than the living room downstairs, though not nearly as messy as the office.

The space wasn't precisely tidy, but its inhabitant was neater than he gave himself credit for.

The loft stretched for what must have been half the length of the house. A spacious, comfy-looking bed occupied a chunk of space on the far side, calling to her. But tempting as it was, in more ways than one, what truly stole Lina's breath was the back wall.

A huge picture window faced the back of the property and Betty's enclosure. Beneath it stood the most inviting window seat she'd ever seen. Piled with squashy pillows, it was practically a daybed. Perfect for stretching out cozily. But that wasn't all—no, the best part framed the window.

Extending out in both directions, lining the walls, were floor-to-ceiling, fully stocked bookshelves.

Was it a library? Was it a bedroom? A bed-brary? Who the hell cared. It was magnificent.

"Shit," she breathed.

He rubbed his neck adorably, appearing bashful and proud at the same time. "Yeah, I like to read."

"I'll say." She stepped closer to the books, shaking her head. "Tony?"

"Hmm?"

She turned to face him. "This is *perfect*."

His resulting grin nearly blinded her.

"'Nothing to worry about,' he says." Lina swatted his arm. "I can't believe you almost kept this from me, you cad!"

Tony laughed heartily. "What can I say? It's a lot to take in. And I know not everyone shares my love of books."

"Those people are not worth considering." She lowered her voice. "And in case you had any doubt, I am *not* one of them."

He leaned in, matching her tone. "I picked up on that."

Up close, his eyes were a lovely, dark chocolate shade. And his lips ... goddess, they were kissable.

But as much as she wanted to do just that, they were in his bedroom, and the way she felt right now, she suspected there'd be no stopping her once she started. There was something about him —her magic shimmered along with the humming pulse deep in her belly, as though, if she didn't know better, it could react to something, some*one*, non-feline. Even though it had never had any connection to her libido. And that should be setting off distant alarm bells… Shouldn't it?

Lina blinked, and forced her attention back to the books. Luckily, there were plenty of them.

Tony followed, stooping to grab a lone apple off the window seat. He tossed it from hand to hand, watching her take in the stacks, before he froze with a strangled noise. He hung his head with a sense of impending doom.

"What is it?"

He glanced up sheepishly. "Tomorrow was supposed to be grocery day. I'm just now realizing what a sad state of affairs my kitchen is in."

"Oh." Hell, she'd be fine with simply that apple, not that she'd admit it. Not yet, anyway.

"I think the best, and probably only, thing I can offer is some leftover Chinese food?" he offered, with a hopeful shrug.

She pretended to consider it. "Does that include chow mein noodles?"

"Yes."

"Dumplings?"

"Naturally."

She nodded sagely. "Then we have a deal, sir."

Tony's smile matched hers, and she was once again distracted by his lips.

So distracted, in fact, that it took her a moment to process when he spoke. "Are you hungry?"

"Hm?" He'd taken the words right out of her mouth. *That's not all he can take from my mouth…*

His eyebrows quirked up before he answered. "I could heat the food up now, if you'd like?"

"Oh. Right. Sure." Her brain finally rallied. "I'd eat it cold, though."

"Tempting, but I run a full-service establishment around here."

"I appreciate that. But admit it, leftovers are even better cold, aren't they?"

He looked as if he wanted to protest, but relented. "Okay, yes. You're right."

"Of course I am. Need any help?"

"I think I can handle it." He squared his shoulders, rising to his full height, all mock imperiousness. "If I leave you here to browse my books while I assemble everything, can I trust you not to snoop anywhere else?"

She flashed him her sauciest smile. "Absolutely not."

Tony snorted. "Figures. Well, I can at least save you some trouble—I don't keep anything valuable in my underwear drawer." He immediately flushed. "I mean— Aw, hell." He gestured to the stairs. "I'm just going to…"

She grinned as she watched him disappear, noting that he moved with fluid grace even when fleeing in embarrassment. She was collecting quite an extensive list of things she liked about Tony Benson. Sparks fizzed deep inside her again, and she found it increasingly difficult to tell whether they resulted from magic-magic, or simply the magic of attraction. With a sigh, she focused her attention on the easiest, and safest, thing to indulge in at the moment—all those books.

What a person read said quite a lot about them, after all.

Tony's collection included a couple of shelves' worth of animal-themed tomes—reference books, training guides, and other various titles related to his work. Even a battered copy of *Winnie-the-Pooh* that made her smile. But when her eyes fell to the set of shelves right next to the window seat, filled with more pulp novels than she'd ever seen, she gasped in delight.

"Oh, Tony, you get more interesting by the moment," she breathed.

Chapter Six

Tony started up the stairs, carefully balancing the tray he'd loaded with their dinner and a bottle of wine. His sense of politeness—along with the fact that he was entertaining a *movie star*—screamed at him to set the dining table, make this a proper date. But some deeper instinct told him that a casual, intimate meal among his books was the better way to go. Lina's fascination with his "library" had ignited a flame of pride in his chest.

Said flame soared into a cheerful blaze when he reached the top step and saw her nestled in a corner of the daybed with one of his paperbacks, one leg tucked up underneath her. She made a near-perfect picture; the only thing missing was a kitten, or seven, cozied up with her. But they could wait. He'd much rather keep her to himself at the moment.

"Hey." His voice came out huskier than he'd expected, and he cleared his throat. "I figured I'd bring dinner up here, if that's all right with you."

Lina's head popped up. "Sure." Her eyes took on a wicked gleam as she brandished the book she held. "Tony Benson, you've been holding out on me."

He frowned in confusion. "What?"

She rose from her seat in one slinky motion and prowled

toward him. "I don't think I've ever seen more Side-of-the-Hill Books outside of a bookstore. Do you have every one they've ever published?"

"Oh, um…" His cheeks heated. "Well, you know…"

"I mean, not only do you have the entire Baking Detective line, which would be impressive on its own. You've also got so many romances!" She waved the book in her hand again. "Do you have any idea how long I've been trying to find *Miss Mott Gets a Scot*? A friend stole mine years ago, and I've never found another copy. It's like my Holy Grail!"

His embarrassment morphed into joy, followed by a resurgence of pride. A startled laugh bubbled up out of him. "I've had that one forever. It might be the first of their romances I ever read. You're welcome to borrow it, if you'd like."

"I would like." She shook her head with a grin. "You have many hidden depths, Mr. Benson."

"I'm glad you think so." He paused. "I'm also glad to find someone who shares my appreciation for the pleasures pulp has to offer."

"Believe me, it has saved me on many an occasion."

Dazzled as he was by her, Tony belatedly realized he still held their dinner tray. He nodded to the window seat. "Shall we?"

Lina returned to her spot, and Tony settled both the tray and himself next to her. He got to work pouring their wine. "Can I let you in on a little secret?" At her enthusiastic nod, he continued, "I also happen to have the follow-up to *Miss Mott*."

Her gorgeous eyes widened. "There was a follow-up?"

"Yep, about her cousin. *Miss Friesian Finds a Parisian*."

She let out an undignified—and utterly charming—snort. "You're pulling my leg."

"I most certainly am not! Here." He handed her a wine glass and stood to scan his shelves. It only took him a moment—unlike his office, these shelves were highly organized. Humming in triumph, he extracted *Miss Friesian* and presented it to Lina with a flourish.

"Stop it." She took the book eagerly and pored over the cover.

He returned to his seat and watched her flip the book over to read its back.

"Okay, this sounds even better than the first one," she said.

"Yeah, I go back and forth over which is my favorite. It changes with my mood."

They grinned at each other and started in on dinner, creating for themselves a lovely indoor picnic of sorts. When he finished his portion of the noodles, he took the paperback from her and started reading it aloud, reveling in her obvious delight.

It took him a few chapters, but he finally got the hang of the leading man's French accent. With an extra flair of gravel in his voice, he read, "'*Ah, you are charming indeed, Mademoiselle Friesian.*'"

So it came as a surprise when Lina reached over and stole the book from his hand. "Okay, that's it. I'm taking over."

"What? Why?"

She shot him an arch look. "That accent?" She shook her head with mock sadness.

"Hey, I was just hitting my stride." He tried to snatch the book back, but she held it firmly out of his reach.

"It was a valiant effort, I'll admit. But I can do these characters far more justice." She placed a less than modest hand over her heart. "I am a professional, after all."

Having far too much fun to even half-heartedly protest her jab at his skill, Tony lifted his hands in surrender. "Then by all means, please proceed."

She nodded regally and began reading. Only a few lines in, he couldn't resist interrupting.

"I'm sorry, but can you remind me, is this chap from Paris ... or Dublin?"

Lina used the paperback to whack him lightly on the arm. "Oh, shut up. I've worked hard to get rid of my lilt, but it still pops up on occasion," she finished with a pout.

"Huh. So it's tricky, even for a professional. Imagine that."

When she narrowed her eyes at him, he responded with an exaggerated, cheeky wink, and they both descended into laughter.

She cleared her throat. "Okay, okay. Let's get back to the story."

Tony grinned as he listened to her rendition—which was, indeed, better than his had been.

"He'd called her charming," she read, *"but as he took her hand and placed a kiss over the back of it, she knew it was he who was the charmer."*

Oh. He'd forgotten that this scene landed so early on in the story. It was tame, as amorous encounters went, but in Lina's husky, expressive voice? He shifted subtly in his seat, his pants feeling tighter already. *Good god, her voice is potent.*

She continued on, oblivious. *"But he wasn't finished. Oh, no, he was every bit the Frenchman, forging a trail of lingering kisses all the way up her arm. Miss Friesian shivered in anticipation."*

Lina's breath hitched, and while it was likely part of her performance, he found himself hoping she was as affected as he was. With her attention trained on the book, he took the opportunity to trail his gaze over the path the Frenchman's mouth currently took with Miss Friesian—up Lina's arm, across her collarbone, and to her mouth.

Her voice deepened further. *"'Do I startle you, Mademoiselle? Or would you like me to continue?'"* She let out a breathless laugh. "Cheeky devil, isn't he?"

Tony smiled, enjoying the fact that, unlike her, he knew what was coming—their intrepid heroine making the "bold" next move of leaning in first for a kiss. "Oh, don't worry. Miss Friesian's got some cheek of her own."

Lina's eyes sparked a fiery gold. "Does she, now? Good for you, Miss F." She bent her head to the page, forgetting in her intrigue to resume reading aloud. Her lips curved into an approving smile—and a lovely blush bloomed up her neck and into her cheeks.

He chuckled to himself, utterly captivated. This was hands-down the best date he'd ever had.

Lina looked back up at him, letting the book fall closed with one finger holding her place. She said quietly, "You know, I think this is the most fun date I've ever had."

Tony laughed heartily. At her quizzical look, he explained, "I was just thinking the exact same thing."

"Were you?"

He hummed his assent—and any remaining simple fun in the air around them evaporated, replaced by a crackling electricity. And an unexpected bout of insecurity on his part. He rubbed at the surprising pressure in his chest.

Unfortunately, Lina noticed. "What is it?" she asked in that throaty purr of hers.

Tony debated the merits of brushing off her question, but instead blurted, "You're a movie star."

She raised one questioning eyebrow. "I am."

"And this is truly a fun date for you?" He gestured around them. "*This*? You must go to all kinds of glamorous parties and dinners."

Her expression softened, her eyes taking on an even brighter sheen. "I do get invited to a lot of those. But more often than not, they feel like work." She reached across the tray to brush her fingers across the back of his hand. "Which is precisely why I'm enjoying myself right now. All *this* is much closer to my idea of a good time."

Tony flipped his hand over and interlaced their fingers, the warmth of her sending a thrill all the way up his arm. His smile spread slowly, and Lina's eyes tracked it, roving hungrily over his mouth. And that sent his lingering restraint up in flames.

He used his free hand to shift a wave of her lustrous brown hair, even softer than he'd imagined, off her face. Her eyes fluttered closed, and she leaned into his touch with a quiet hum. The move was so much like one of his cats, he almost laughed. Except his cats had never made him feel like this.

Closing the distance between them, he whispered her name against her lips, attempting to start out soft, slow. But the meeting of their mouths was like flint to tinder, and she greedily opened to him with a low moan. He responded by sliding his tongue against hers. She tasted like wine, and something else, something uniquely her, and the recipe set his entire body buzzing.

Needing more, he moved closer, but his knee bumped against the dinner tray, and the rattling of the dishes brought a small shred of common sense back to him. He tore himself away and quickly moved the tray to a nearby table, then slid himself next to her.

They crashed together with record speed. Lina's hands dove into his hair, her fingernails raking across his scalp and enticing a growl from his throat. He pulled her closer, gripping the lush, perfect curves of her waist.

He completely lost track of time, losing himself in her instead. When she crawled into his lap with a purr, he kissed his way across her jaw with an amused hum. Her motion had caused the hem of her soft sweater to ride up, and he took full advantage, sliding his hands under it, over her even softer skin. She gasped at the contact, the sound speaking right to his already eager cock.

"I should probably tell you," he said between kisses, working his way up to the silky patch of skin behind her ear. "I don't usually move this fast." He took her earlobe gently between his teeth. "I'm usually much more of a…" When she ground her hips against his lap, he nearly lost his train of thought. "…gentleman."

Her chuckle was low and raspy. "You're pacing yourself just fine, sir." She pulled his head down to dive into his mouth for a long, wonderful minute. When she finally broke off to look him in the eye, she appeared as dazed as he felt. "There's just something about you." She kissed him again. "About me when I'm with you." Another kiss.

"About *us*," he added.

Lina nodded, her smile more seductive than ever. His hands drifted as far as the underside of her breasts, his thumbs skimming along the satiny edge of her brassiere. That touch seemed to rob her of what little patience she had, for she grabbed the edge of her sweater and pulled it up and off in one swift movement.

With a groan, Tony took in the gorgeous swell of her breasts, her nipples visibly rising beneath the fabric. He bent his head to kiss his way down her collarbone and lick between her cleavage.

"Hell, Tony," she breathed. Her head lolled back, even as she blindly went to work on the buttons of his shirt.

Her hot fingertips skimmed over his chest, leaving a trail of fire in their wake, and he closed his teeth in a gentle bite over the top of one breast, reveling as she purred once more in response. She'd just begun to slide his shirt off his shoulders when a guttural, moaning cry rent the air, simultaneously ghost-like and rumbling. But this noise hadn't come from her.

They stared at each other in surprise, as the sound echoed a second time. Tony blinked, realizing with a start that it was Betty. Lina must have come to the same conclusion, and the two of them burst into laughter.

She shot a glance over his shoulder, and Tony twisted his head to follow her gaze. The window behind them overlooked the leopard enclosure, a fact he'd conveniently forgotten. Betty currently faced away from the house.

"Oh dear, can she see us from there? Did we disturb her?" Lina asked breathlessly.

He snorted. "I doubt she thinks you're mauling me. That was hardly a distress cry."

"Well, of course not. It sounded like a mating call."

No, that couldn't be.

Lina grimaced as she added, "Shit, did we send her into heat?"

"Yes, because watching humans engaged in erotic activity is a known turn-on for leopards."

She narrowed her eyes at his dry tone, and their gazes locked in mock challenge for a long moment before they broke and collapsed against each other, mirth overtaking them.

"Yep, definitely the most fun," she said, her breath tickling his chest.

He sucked in a sharp inhale, and she pulled back to meet his eyes, the air sparking around them all over again. Lina traced the top edge of his chest hair, making him shiver.

"Do you need to check on Betty?" she whispered.

He should probably keep an eye on her in the coming days, especially with Bob around, but he didn't want to think about that at the moment. "Not right now."

Lina abandoned his chest to trail her finger over his lips. "Do you want to…" Her breath audibly hitched when he darted his tongue out to lick her. "…stop what we were doing?"

"I do not." He closed his teeth in a gentle bite over her finger. "Do you?"

One side of her mouth lifted seductively. "No."

She closed the distance for a kiss and slid his shirt the rest of the way down his arms. Once he was free of it, Tony reached behind him to tug the curtains closed. Lina raised an eyebrow.

He shrugged in response. "Just in case."

Her chuckle turned into an appreciative hum as her eyes raked over his now completely bared torso. He'd never thought of himself as more than average, but the way she looked at him, like she wanted to devour him… It made him want to preen for her. He pulled her closer, delving into her mouth while his hands skated across the warm skin of her back.

When Lina returned her hands to his hair, he let out a satisfied groan. In return, he began to explore her, sliding one palm down to her lush ass and the other up to caress one of her breasts. It filled his grasp perfectly, and he couldn't resist rubbing his thumb across her nipple, eliciting a hiss from her.

Lina danced her hips over his lap, and before long she was riding him with expert precision.

"Wait," he rasped, both hands gripping her hips, holding her still. "I won't last this way…" Her perfect mouth twisted into a pout, and he chuckled. "I didn't say I was going to leave you hanging, did I?" He punctuated his admonishment with a gentle bite to her lower lip.

"Oh?" She managed to infuse that one syllable with both arch inquiry and a moan of pleasure, and holy hell, was she magnificent.

He answered her with a deep kiss, then teased at the waist-band of her trousers for a few moments before twisting the top hook open. She practically growled when he slid his hand inside, fingertips grazing through her curls before venturing lower.

"Already so wet," he whispered against her mouth.

Her satisfied, rumbling purr had already begun when he found her clit; at his gentle flick, it transformed into a mewl of pure desire. So when she suddenly rose from his lap, he was more than a bit surprised.

Until she locked her gaze on his, kicked off her shoes, and proceeded to slide her pants and silky underwear down her legs in one fluid motion.

"Fuck." His curse, low and guttural, set off sparks in her eyes. He allowed himself a moment to take in her beauty, her stunning, soft curves.

Desire zinged through him, fueling his need to match her boldness. Before she could step closer to him, he swung his legs up and reclined fully on the window seat. He rubbed at his jaw, then tapped his chin.

"Have a seat."

GODDESSES ABOVE. All sensation rushed to her core, leaving nothing remaining for her legs. She wobbled a bit. *He did just offer you a solution to that problem…*

She needed a second to catch her breath. Marshall her thoughts. Or something. She wasn't entirely sure she remembered her own name.

It was all too much. Almost.

Tony Benson was one hell of a danger. Typically, when she got involved with anyone, she kept things casual. Much easier that way, given the part of her she didn't—couldn't—share with anyone.

The part of her that was, somehow, gaining momentum by the second. Not that she was at any risk of shifting—goddess, that would be a disaster, if her magic worked that way. But enough of her power called to her now; she felt it sparking invisibly beneath her skin, and hoped it stayed that way. Despite her bravado, she was finding it increasingly difficult to keep a lid on.

Tony had blown right past all her defenses, in a way she'd never experienced before. She—*and* her magic—wanted him so fucking much.

He lounged there, all glorious invitation and glowing skin. The way his pants tented must be agonizing for him, yet he focused his attention solely on her. Kept rubbing at his mouth, as if he was starving for her…

And that commanding tone in his voice. *Bloody hell.*

Defenses be damned. If her magic wanted her to do this, who was she to deny it? Thinking was highly overrated anyway.

"If you insist," she rasped, not sure if she was answering his earlier command or herself. Something in her voice had him biting his lip, which was unfair. That was *her* job.

She found enough strength in her legs to slink gracefully to the window seat and straddle his lap. Unable to resist, she bent to his mouth, taking that bite. He groaned, letting her have her fill before regaining control. He grasped her waist and pulled his head back, gaze full of fire.

"That's not the seat I meant," he growled.

He tugged her hips toward him while sliding himself down, until he had her positioned where he wanted her—where she *needed* to be—hovering and ready to sit on his face.

His breath was hot against her skin, sending her soaring already, but she arched an eyebrow and asked, "Better?"

Tony simply chuckled in response, and she felt the delicious rumble of it…

"Oh goddess," she cried out, as he slowly dragged his tongue over her. He finished with a fluttering against her clit that matched what he'd done earlier with his finger. She'd always been sensitive, but he drove her higher, faster.

He let out an appreciative hum, then his restraint snapped. His grip on her hips tightened as he held her against his face, suddenly devouring. His lips and tongue and teeth worked relentlessly, yet she couldn't get enough. She shot her arm out to brace herself, palm slamming against the side of the bookshelf.

Her other hand tangled in the soft waves of his hair. If the feral sound he let out was any indication, it seemed to drive him wild when she ran her fingers through it. *Good.* She gripped harder, wanting to give him back a fraction of the blind desire he stoked in her.

As his tongue worked inside her, she realized rather belatedly that she could give him a hell of a lot more than a fraction.

It killed her to pause for even a second—she was close, so close. But she unearthed the willpower to tug insistently on his hair. "Wait," she bit out. "Hold on."

Tony tore his mouth from her without hesitation and looked up, lips glistening and eyes filled with concern. "Are you all right?" he panted.

"I am. But you're not."

Confusion flitted across his face, but she couldn't afford to answer him. She needed to move quickly, to hold onto that glorious pleasure throbbing between her legs. Space was tight, but she pivoted to straddle him in the opposite direction. Her hands fell to the waistband of his pants, and she threw a glance over her shoulder.

"This okay?" She hoped she sounded more seductive than desperate.

Either way, it worked for him, because his slightly dazed expression sharpened. He licked his lips hungrily and nodded.

She shoved his pants past his thighs and freed his cock, but didn't have more than a second of greedy appreciation before he yanked her hips down, returning her to his face. She practically shrieked his name as he went to work again.

Two could play at that game.

Lina wasted no time teasing him as she'd normally like to—instead she tightened her fingers around the base of his cock and sucked hard on the head. His hips jerked up and his moan reverberated inside her. Through the sparks of her own pleasure, she recognized how close he was. She licked at the bead of salty moisture leaking from him, and began to move, matching the slide of her lips to the rhythm of his tongue.

His movements became increasingly erratic, as did hers. Desire overflowed in one endless, magical wave. Her legs shook where they bracketed his head, but he held her steady. One last, hard suck on her clit, and she was done. Golden fireworks burst behind her eyelids, and it was entirely possible that some also sparkled visibly around them, but she was too elated to care anymore. She screamed around his cock, the animalistic sound rivaling the call they'd heard from the yard, and clenched him like a vise with both her lips and her fingers.

Beneath her other hand, his thigh muscles tightened, harder than a rock, as he attempted to hold himself back until she came down. Wanting him to join her in her sated haze, she increased her pressure, gently biting him as she dragged her lips up his length.

The hot jet hit the back of her throat, but she didn't have time to dwell on the sensation, because his shout of satisfaction set off a sequel to her orgasm—quieter this time, but plenty devastating.

Beneath her, Tony melted into the seat, and gently eased his face from under her. Lina, in turn, collapsed over him, her forehead pressing against the coarse hair on his upper thigh. They panted together blissfully for several, gradually slowing heartbeats, and then she rolled herself off him.

Their eyes finally met over the length of each other's bodies, small smiles blooming into matching grins.

"Still the most fun?" he asked playfully, his voice hoarse.

She laughed through her nod. He jumped up to gather a washcloth from the bathroom, but by the time he returned, a bit of her glow had dimmed, replaced by an unexpected round of doubts—some she'd thought long-buried, others brand new and unique to Tony.

He hadn't run screaming in fear, which meant he likely hadn't noticed any errant magic escaping her—or clocked that she'd sounded far too much like his beloved leopard as she came; her cheeks flushed in embarrassment as she thought about it now. But the fact remained, her hidden side had been very much present. Not only present—close to being in control of her, rather than the other way around. She hadn't felt so near to losing that control since she'd been a girl, first learning to wield the power inside her. And especially not since she'd let it go practically dormant in the years since she left Ireland, and that life, behind.

Lina didn't know what was more worrying—her magic's unforeseen, near-frightening connection to her attraction to Tony, or just how much she'd liked it.

He must have noticed her sudden introspection, because he paused his gentle ministrations. "Hey. You okay?"

She wasn't entirely certain, and she sure as hell couldn't be honest as to why.

Lina scooted to a seated position, focusing on the one excuse for her mood that she could explain. All magic aside, a doubt she didn't realize she still harbored had resurfaced along with the rest. "I am. I guess I just…" His eyes held nothing but tenderness, and she so wished she could tell him the full truth. She at least admitted, "You said it yourself. I'm a movie star. And as bold as I am, I'm hardly the characters I play. I suppose I'm only hoping…"

"That I'm not disappointed by the real thing?" he prompted softly.

She nodded, avoiding his eyes. "It's silly, I know."

"No, it's not." His fingers grazed her cheek, before he gently lifted her chin. "You might be a movie star, and one I confess I've had a bit of a crush on for a while." He traced his thumb over her bottom lip, and she shivered. "But the extraordinary, perfect evening I'm having? That's because of *you*, Lina. Not your characters. The woman I've gotten to know over the last, admittedly few, days."

Warmth settled in her chest, and she grinned. She might not have said everything she wanted to, but he'd taken in her smaller doubt, found the seed of good in it and nurtured it, returning it back to her in the loveliest way. No wonder she was falling so hard already.

He kissed her, and she leaned into him, letting go of her worry about the huge part of her he still did not, in fact, know. Instead, for the first time in her adult life, she was sorely tempted to let someone in on her secret. This someone might actually be worthy of it.

Dangerous indeed.

Chapter Seven

*L*ina was spared from thinking too much about her predicament over the following week, owing in part to her busy filming schedule, and much more to Betty's rapidly approaching audition. Tony was hard at work polishing his leopard's performance skills ahead of her big day, and while he was reluctant to admit it, Lina could tell his nerves threatened to get the better of him.

She tried to reassure him during their frequent phone calls. And though they'd only managed to schedule one additional date, she was rather proud of the way she'd distracted him on that occasion. Their inability to keep their hands off one another had most assuredly given them both a reprieve from lingering worries.

Luckily, Betty's audition coincided with her day off, so Lina eagerly headed out to the sanctuary. Tony hadn't come right out and asked, but she suspected he'd appreciate the moral support. She wanted to cheer Betty on as well.

When they'd spoken early the day before, he'd been in good spirits, and positive about his and Betty's chances. So when she arrived at Applegate, it came as a bit of a shock to find him pacing in front of the enclosure, running both hands through his hair.

"Tony? Is everything okay?"

He raised wild, frantic eyes to her. "Lina, thank god it's just you." She'd barely opened her mouth to answer when he threw his arms around her. "I don't know what I'm going to do."

"What's wrong?"

"It's Betty."

Her stomach dropped. "What happened? Is she hurt?"

Tony let go of her and heaved a sigh. "No, nothing like that. Physically, she's just fine."

She blinked up at him in confusion. "But…?"

He gestured behind him, ushering her toward the enclosure. "Come see for yourself."

When she glanced around him, she didn't see the problem at first. Betty lay on the ground, her head resting on her crossed front paws. Lina thought she might be asleep, until the leopard lifted her head listlessly and speared her with the saddest, most heartsick look in her golden eyes.

"Oh," she breathed.

"She's been like this since last night," Tony said, his voice threaded with worry. "Just lying there, all lethargic. I've tried everything, but I can't snap her out of it."

Lina took a few steps closer, tentatively reaching her hand through the bars to brush the top of Betty's head. All she got in response was a small, rumbling huff. Betty didn't even lift her head again.

"What's the matter, girl?" she whispered, massaging Betty gently.

"I wish I knew," Tony quietly responded on Betty's behalf.

Lina glanced over her shoulder at him, without breaking contact with the leopard. Tony looked nearly as miserable as Betty.

"She's barely touched any food, isn't responding to her favorite toys. She won't even get up, let alone do any of the tricks we've practiced." He scrubbed a hand through his hair, leaving it standing on end. "And she's gotten so good at them all, too."

Lina turned back to Betty and sent a pulse of her calming magic through her fingertips. She tried to keep it small enough to be invisible to the naked eye, but decided to distract Tony with talk, just in case.

"Is it something she ate? Before she stopped, that is."

He shook his head and started pacing again. "No. That's the thing. The minute she started acting funny, Carl gave her a thorough checkup. He couldn't find a thing wrong with her. Nothing obvious, anyway."

"So whatever it is, it's her spirit. Poor thing."

She checked to make sure Tony was still in anxious motion, distracted, before reaching her free hand to Betty as well. Without knowing the specifics of what was wrong, her magic would be less targeted, and therefore less effective. Her attention caught on the other corner of the enclosure—currently sitting empty.

"Where's Bob?"

"Those jackasses from the circus came for him yesterday." His mouth twisted into an angry grimace. "When I was out getting supplies. I didn't even get the chance to argue for keeping him here. Carl maintains there would've been nothing I could do, but still." Tony paused, shoulders slumped. "And then Betty…"

"Oh, I'm sorry." One more look at Betty, and understanding dawned. "Well, no wonder."

"What?"

Lina shot him a look. "Tony." At his continued obtuseness, she gestured to the heartsick leopard. "She misses Bob."

"I hardly think that's it…" His eyebrows furrowed as he considered it. "No, they haven't spent all that much time together."

"You could say the same about us."

Tony's face softened at her saucy smirk. "True. But we're people. Leopards don't form attachments like that."

"Not in the wild. But…"

He shook his head and resumed pacing. "Nah. It's definitely

something more than that." An anxious hand raked his scalp again. "If only we had time to figure it out…"

Lina wanted to argue, but sensed she'd never get through to him while he was in this state. Besides, he did have a point about timing. They couldn't get Betty's buddy back before the audition, so they needed a temporary, and immediate, fix.

With Tony still in motion, she returned both her hands to Betty's soft pelt. Lina didn't know much about mending a broken heart, but she focused as much energy as she could on what she remembered of general healing, sending all her calm and affection for Betty—and Betty's keeper—into her touch.

Sparks fired throughout her body, gathering and coalescing into a solid, steady warmth in her palms and fingertips. *Come on, lass. Let's get you feeling better. For yourself, but also for Tony.*

Betty let out a rumbling purr, but otherwise made no signs of rallying. Lina *was* soothing her, she could tell. Just not enough. But she couldn't risk doing more with Tony right there.

Hmm. Maybe that's part of the problem.

She reluctantly let go of Betty and turned to him. Sensing her attention, he stopped in his tracks and stared at her. The poor man looked positively green.

"Lina, *what* am I going to do?" he hissed. "Nick and the others will be here any minute now, expecting us to perform."

She wished her magic worked on humans as well. "I'm sure they'll understand. Animals can be unpredictable, everyone knows that."

"But I've promised them she won't be. I'm trying to convince everyone that I'm the guy who can make even wild animals predictable, capable of acting, doing shit on cue. And if I can't deliver, what does that say about me?" He spread his arms to take in their surroundings. "About what I'm trying to do here? No one will take me seriously, and then I won't be able to help any of my animals, or get Bob back. I won't be able to help her." He finished with a helpless glance at Betty.

She rested her hand on his shoulder. "Tony, that's not going to happen."

"How do you know?"

"Because I've seen you with your critters. And anyone who spends even five minutes watching you together knows how good you are with them. How much you care for them."

He exhaled slowly. "But Betty ... I've known her since she was a tiny cub. I know her better than anyone ever could. Why can't I figure out how to help her now? She's so damn sad."

Lina's heart broke for him. "I don't know. But..." She paused, weighing her words, trying to find a way to voice her theory without hurting him further. "It might be possible that your ... worry ... isn't exactly the best thing for her at the moment?" She bit her lip, watching as her words sank in.

Tony opened his mouth to respond, closing it again immediately. "Oh." He tried to speak a few more times, before finally raising anguished eyes to hers. "You think I'm making her feel worse?"

"No, not necessarily." She squeezed his shoulder. "It's only, you two are so connected. Maybe she's picking up on your nervousness, on top of feeling poorly herself, and it's all snow-balling."

Plus, with him hovering and pacing, she'd never be able to risk using more of her magic on Betty.

He nodded. "That does make sense."

She cupped his face in both hands. "Tony, I know it's easy for me to say, but I truly believe it's all going to be okay. Yes, you have a lot riding on this. But you are good at what you do." She smirked. "And trust me. I've worked with human actors who were far more temperamental than Betty's being right now. Nick and the others *are* going to understand."

That got a chuckle out of him, finally. She could feel his tension gradually ebbing. With a sigh, he leaned his forehead against hers.

"Thanks, Lina."

"Any time."

After a few moments, Tony straightened and squared his shoulders. "So. The audition might not be the end of the world." He glanced at Betty again. "But I'm still worried. I've never seen her like this."

She started to respond with a quip about Tony's apparent cynicism over true leopard love, when the high-pitched cry of a nearby hawk pierced the air. It relieved her tremendously to see the sound's calming effect on Tony.

"Wait for it," he said, in a hushed tone.

Sure enough, an answering call echoed, and Lina spotted two hawks swooping low among the trees edging the property. The corners of Tony's mouth actually kicked up.

"They are a mated pair. I've always loved not only that they found each other, but also that they call this area home. They might not need our care, but I'd like to think…"

"They approve of what you're building here?"

A wash of pink rose in his cheeks, but his smile held. "Yeah."

She returned his grin, thrilled to see his mood so improved—and that he could still recognize some forms of love after all. They heard another cry, and the shadow of one of the birds, flying even closer this time, passed over Tony. Followed by a flash of something that looked an awful lot like…

Oh, no.

Practically in slow motion, Tony turned his head, eyes wide with dawning horror, as he took in his shoulder and upper arm. Where several large spots of hawk shit now resided.

Lina raised her hands to her mouth, trying valiantly to stifle a giggle. The whole thing would, under normal circumstances, be highly comical. But one look at Tony's face, and her laugh died in her throat. All the calm he'd managed to claw back evaporated quickly.

His mouth gaped open, lips simultaneously curling in disgust. A choked sound escaped his throat.

She risked another look at his shirt, and … it was truly a huge stain, wasn't it? "Oh, dear."

Tony raised his eyes—carefully—to the heavens. He could have just as easily been talking to the hawks or a higher power when he shouted, "Are you shitting me?"

Lina couldn't stop her snort this time. At Tony's disbelieving look, she held up a hand. "I'm sorry, it's only… I think that might be the first time I've heard someone ask that question when the answer was actually, quite literally, *yes*." She bit her lip in an effort to contain another laugh.

He seemed to hover on the border between agitation and giving in to the laughter himself, but unfortunately, another glance at his arm sent him in the wrong direction. He hung his head with a wheezing groan.

She needed to salvage this, and fast. "You know, lots of people consider it a sign of good luck, being shat on by a bird." It came out as more of a question than she'd intended. Warding off his argument, she soldiered on. "You did admit you want the hawks to approve of you. Think of this as their blessing."

"They couldn't've just left it at a verbal endorsement?" His melodic voice spiked into shrill territory by the finish. Then he split a frantic glare between Betty and the front of the property. "Oh, god. I can't meet a bunch of Hollywood bigwigs looking like this." He gestured wildly at his arm.

He was swiftly working himself back up to a million.

"Tony." She took hold of his face again, since that had helped so much earlier. "You need to breathe." She cut off his protest. "I mean it. Take a deep breath. Right now." She watched as he did, nodding. "That's it. Now listen to me. First, you have to go up to the house and change."

His eyes darted in Betty's direction. "But—"

"But nothing. You said it yourself, you can't meet anyone looking like that. Go put on a clean shirt, and I'll stay here with Betty."

That, at least, seemed to reassure him. "I guess so."

She stroked her thumbs over his cheeks. "Trust me. She and I are great pals, remember?" His jaw relaxed a bit under her hands. "Let me see if I can give her a pep talk. Actor-to-actor."

He melted further at that, much to her gratification. "Okay," he murmured. "Okay."

Lina pressed a kiss to his lips. "Everything's going to be just fine, Tony."

He nodded briskly, coming back to himself. "Thanks."

She took him by the shoulders and turned him in the direction of the house, giving him a soft shove. "Go."

Thankfully, he obeyed. But Lina's heart sank all over again when she faced Betty. She shook her head. What a pair these two made.

"Okay, lady. Now it's your turn."

She laid both hands on Betty once more. Closing her eyes and inhaling deeply, she channeled all her magic, all of herself, into the leopard. She was more convinced than ever that Betty's low spirits had everything to do with Bob, though she was less than sure how to form her power into a Band-Aid for the heart. Perhaps if she used it more often, if she'd gone through more training. Chosen this path in life.

But there was no time for introspection now. She'd simply have to do the best she could with what healing she could manage, pushing every bit of calm and uplift she had at her disposal into the cat. The tingling sparks in her body coalesced into a pleasant burn that crested in her hands and ebbed into the leopard.

Just as before, Betty rumbled her appreciation for the soothing energy, but failed to get up. Lina dropped her hands with a sigh. "Come on, love. Can't you manage just a trick or two? For our Tony? Hell, even standing up would be something, honey."

Betty simply looked at her with that sad expression in her beautiful eyes.

Lina bit her lip. What more could she do? She'd done everything in her power…

Not everything.

She gasped at the sudden, wild idea. *No, I couldn't. Could I?*

No. It was ridiculous. Alice would surely disapprove. It was just the kind of reckless, impulsive idea she'd had all the time as a teenager, the attitude that likely had her elders sighing in relief when she'd left this life behind. But she desperately wanted to help both Betty and Tony. And this *would* be helping…

Suddenly remembering that Tony's loft faced this area, she glanced over her shoulder. The sun reflected off the window, making it difficult to see much of anything inside. She rubbed a fingernail along her lower lip, debating. *I really shouldn't…*

Another look at sweet Betty, so dejected, and… Lina groaned, approaching the enclosure.

"I am so going to regret this, aren't I?" she muttered.

Chapter Eight

Tony carefully peeled his shirt off and tossed it on the floor in front of his laundry hamper. He hoped it wasn't completely ruined—he rather liked its muted geometric pattern—but stain removal was the very least of his worries.

Following Lina's sage advice, he took another long, deep breath, steadfastly ignoring his picture window. She was right; he was no help to Betty in his panicked state. And watching her mope outside while he changed would only agitate him all over again.

Focusing on what he could control, he pulled open his wardrobe door, perused his selection of clean shirts, and chose one in a warm mustard color. Not his favorite, but it would do—it was, after all, mercifully free of bird shit. He slipped it on, taking his time doing up the buttons while willing his nerves to remain steady.

The executives will understand. And if Lina does manage to lift Betty's spirits, you'll need to lead her through the routine. Be calm. Commanding. You can do this.

It took a few minutes, but he finally felt Lina's optimism sinking in.

The sight of himself in the mirror made him grimace. His hair was always the first casualty of his agitation, so he grabbed a comb and attempted to calm the havoc he'd wreaked. It occurred to him that he should perhaps add a tie to his outfit, lend himself an extra air of professionalism, but he rejected the notion almost immediately. Anything hanging from his neck was asking for trouble when it came to animals, even one as devoted to him as Betty.

No. He inhaled sharply. *She'll be fine. Whatever this is, it's just a temporary setback.*

A flash of something out the window caught his eye, as if a small cloud had just flitted across the bright sunlight streaming in. *Odd.* It had been perfectly clear all day. He risked a look, and the light was bright enough that he had to blink a few times to bring the enclosure into focus. Neither Betty nor Lina was visible from his position, but the glare outside stung his eyes, making Bob's former corner look like it wavered a bit.

See, that's what you get for looking.

As Tony straightened up, he noticed several of the pillows dotting the seat were still somewhat crushed from his and Lina's interlude there. The heated reminder made him smile genuinely for the first time all day. When the dust finally settled, he couldn't wait to explore what else they could do to each other in that space.

All he had to do was get through the next hour.

He forced himself back down the stairs, debating how soon he should warn Nick and the others about Betty. Before he'd reached a decision, however, he stepped out his front door to find their car pulling up.

"Tony, hello!" Nick called out as he hopped out of the driver's seat.

Tony waved in response, fighting down a new surge of anxiety.

Nick led the introductions as two more men emerged from the car—a tall, friendly-looking British chap named Colin, who was apparently the screenwriter; and the more serious, but still amiable Mr. Peabody, the director.

"Welcome, gentlemen." Tony's voice came out steady, much to his relief.

"This is quite the setup you've got here," Peabody said.

"Thank you." He gestured to the stables. "Why don't you come through here? I'll show you a bit of our facilities on our way out back."

He might be throwing caution to the wind, but he kept mum about Betty for the moment, instead focusing on the mini-tour and his other, non-feline animals. On the off chance Lina had gotten through to Betty in some way, these guys didn't need to know about their rocky morning.

And if a disastrous wreck awaited, he wanted to delay the inevitable as long as possible.

The men were sufficiently impressed by the tour, though Nick gave Rupert a wide berth, mumbling something about an unfortunate incident the one time he'd acted with a monkey. Colin flashed the star an amused, quizzical look, but Tony's nerves kept him from being too curious himself.

Clearly eager to change the subject, Nick rubbed his hands together. "So, when do we get to meet this illustrious leopard of yours?"

"Right. Of course." Tony pasted what he hoped was an encouraging smile on his face. "This way." He held his breath as they exited the building, fully prepared to start tap dancing the minute they saw Betty in all her melancholic glory.

He stopped short when he took in the scene before him.

Betty lounged on top of her little cave, tail swishing playfully, just as she had when he'd first introduced her to Lina. As soon as she spotted the group, she leapt gracefully down from her perch and sauntered to the fence, before sitting on her hind quarters and tilting her head with an extra glint in her eyes.

Tony blinked, barely refraining from uttering a "thank fuck" aloud. He glanced around, but Lina had disappeared, probably wanting to avoid distracting her colleagues. Which was rather unfortunate, as Tony wanted to kiss her senseless in gratitude for whatever she'd done to rally Betty.

"Oh, she's a beauty," Peabody murmured.

"She is," Nick agreed, and let out a low whistle. "Look at those eyes. Really lures you in like a noir dame, doesn't she?"

Colin chuckled as he chimed in, "She's a sultry one. I can definitely write some fun into the script for her."

Betty positively preened under their attention, and Tony felt dizzy with emotional whiplash. But exhilarating relief was a hell of a lot better than the alternative, so he snapped to attention, slipping into his role as trainer and beginning the speech he was now very glad he'd rehearsed so many times.

"Fellas, I'd like you to meet Betty, my pride and joy." He stood in front of them and raised a cautioning hand. "I'd ask that you do give her a little distance, especially to start. I assure you, she is more sweetheart than femme fatale, and as docile as a wild animal can be. But she is still just that—a wild animal. As you're strangers to her, it's best to let her get accustomed to your presence slowly."

The three men nodded, and Tony appreciated how seriously they took the situation. As he approached Betty, disbelief nagged at him. She was acting like a completely different animal than she'd been not even an hour ago.

He squinted. Come to think of it, she *looked* a little different too. *Were her spots always laid out in that pattern?*

Tony bit back a groan. The stress had done more of a number on him than he'd realized if he was imagining rearranged spots.

Betty tilted her head to one side, almost warily, as if she, too, analyzed his mental state. *Great, even my leopard thinks I'm losing it.*

He cleared his throat. "Betty, love. These are the gents I was telling you about. Are you ready to impress them?"

She dipped her head, and … looked up at them through her lashes … *like some kind of coquette?*

It earned her laughs from the assembled group. Tony swallowed. He'd have to unpack her newfound sauciness later.

"Right. Let's get started, shall we?" He picked up the pail of Betty's treats and entered the enclosure. "Okay, girl. You can do this. *We* can do this," he finished under his breath.

For her part, Betty continued … really, flirting was the only way to describe it. She was *flirting* with their audience, and he held in an astonished chuckle at the sight.

"All right, Betty, how about a little fetch?" Oddly, she made no reaction to him. "Betty?" Still nothing, as if she didn't recognize her own name.

Nick and Colin remained too fascinated by her to notice, but Peabody eyed Tony with a hint of skepticism. His nerves threatened, but he took a calming breath and tried again, infusing his voice with every bit of command he could muster. "Betty."

It worked. His leopard's head whipped around, an almost sheepish look crossing her face. She turned her body to face him fully, sitting on her haunches at full attention. Ready for him. He exhaled in relief.

Lifting her rope toy above his head, just as he had in front of Lina, Tony took Betty through a couple of rounds of fetch. She sailed through the exercise gracefully.

Tossing her a treat, Tony said, "Good girl."

He watched in fascination as a shiver rippled through her sleek body at his praise. She regarded him with a fiery cast to her golden eyes that he'd never seen before. It almost reminded him of the way Lina looked at him, which was ridiculous, he knew. But god, the reminder of her made him want to kiss his gratitude into her even more.

He guided Betty through more of her small arsenal of tricks, to the delight of their assembled audience. Much to his own delight —and significant surprise, given how the day started—Betty nailed every bit of their act with flair.

When they reached the grand finale, where Betty stood on her hind legs, he almost stopped, not wanting to push her too far. But she'd more than earned his confidence, so he put his trust in his leopard. She rose up, her slight wobbling almost looking as if it was for show, rather than due to any lack of balance. Tony didn't have time to analyze it, however, because Betty proceeded to take first one step, then another.

He staggered back on one foot, his own wobbliness every bit real. Remembering their audience, he recovered quickly and moved backward with more intention, leading her a few more steps.

She dropped back down on all fours, and elation and shock rocked through him in equal measure—as much progress as they'd made lately, she'd only managed *one* step on her best day.

"Well done, Betty." He bent to rub her head, and she melted into his hand. "You were perfect, sweetheart." He'd never felt prouder.

And honestly, a little unsettled as well. He couldn't shake the sense that Betty had stopped flirting with their audience and started flirting with *him*. Even stranger—he'd…liked it?

He was going to have one hell of a headache once he got through this afternoon.

"Are we allowed to applaud?" Nick asked in a stage-whisper.

Tony chuckled, thankful to the man for pulling him back to the present. "A little bit won't hurt."

The three of them clapped, quietly but heartily. Betty, in turn, padded right up to the fence and dropped into what could only be called a four-legged version of a curtsy. Tony let out a huff of laughter. He had no idea when she'd become such a ham, but it was clear she'd found her true calling.

Not that he was about to complain.

He tossed Betty one more treat before making his way out of the enclosure. She pounced on it, as she had with her others, but as he fastened the latch on the gate, he noticed something odd. Almost surreptitiously, Betty added the bit of meat to a small pile, tucked under a clump of leaves. *Saving them for later? Or is there something wrong with her digestion after all?* Either way, her behavior was unusual to say the least.

Adding to the resurgence of his worries, Nick and the others had turned to confer with each other in hushed tones. They'd clearly been impressed, and Betty had more than nailed her routine—she'd performed even better than he'd expected her to before her alarming mood swing. But given their initial hesitation over casting a leopard in the first place, Tony had no idea if Betty's stellar performance would be enough to sell them.

He set the treat bucket down and steeled himself. His guests broke apart at the same moment, and he held his breath. But they were on him in an instant, extending their hands congenially.

"Well, I'm sold," Nick assured him.

The other two nodded, and Tony fought back an exhilarated whoop, wanting to appear professional.

"Say, that was even more impressive than I expected," Colin offered warmly.

"It was," Peabody replied. "A part of me is still a little unsure about a leopard. But she's an impressive one, and we could make it work. Though I'd like to see how she does in front of cameras, with more people around."

"Of course," Tony agreed.

"But if that goes well," the director continued, "we might be able to make this little lady a star."

"That's wonderful. Thank you."

The trio didn't have time to linger, so Tony ushered them back to their car.

Nick opened the driver's side door and leaned his elbow on it. "I don't mean to rush things, but how would you feel about giving Betty that screen test in a few days? Are you familiar with Ransom Ranch?"

"The movie place? Oh, sure. It's just a couple miles from here."

"That's the one. Phoenix is renting it out right now for a western. Since all the equipment will already be there, why don't we bring you over? It'll save you having to transport Betty all the way into Hollywood, not yet anyway."

"Good idea," Peabody added. "Probably a more familiar environment for Betty, too, and fewer people around than at the studio."

"That sounds perfect," Tony said. Lina had been right; this group understood a lot. "It will be beneficial to everyone to transition Betty into this in smaller steps. If you decide to go with her, of course," he tacked on.

Peabody nodded briskly, then turned to Nick. "And let's see about getting Miss Leonard out for it as well, for a chemistry test. She is comfortable working with a jungle cat, yes?"

"You bet."

"She's already met Betty, as a matter of fact," Tony chimed in. "They hit it off beautifully."

"Excellent," Peabody replied.

Much more transparent than the director, Nick shot Tony a delighted expression. "I'll have someone call you to arrange all the details. Thanks again, Tony. Truly impressive stuff. Assuming all the rest goes well, we're looking forward to working with you. And Betty."

"Us, too."

Despite Peabody's reticence, Nick's enthusiasm was infectious and gave him real hope. They said their goodbyes, and Tony forced himself to calmly watch them depart, rather than dancing a jig right there in the driveway. One of the hawks screeched in the distance.

"Guess that shit really was good luck," he snickered.

Once the coast was clear, he whirled around with an extra flourish, and took off to find Lina and give Betty extra belly rubs.

He nearly ran into Lina outside the back doorway of the stables.

"Lina! We did it!" Unable to help himself, he yanked her into his arms, twirling her around.

She let out a sound that was half-yelp, half-laugh.

He held her tight for a long, glorious moment. "You were right. I think it's all going to be okay."

"Told you so," she murmured against his shoulder.

"I don't know what you said to Betty, but whatever it was, you're a genius!" He captured her mouth in an exhilarating kiss. "You should've seen her. She was magnificent. Where did you go, by the way? Did you sneak back to the house to let Betty have her moment?"

"Something like that," she said breathlessly. "I'm so happy for you, Tony."

"Listen, I have every intention of expressing my gratitude to you properly." The sexy curve of her lips beckoned him in for another quick kiss. "But I should probably give my other gal a little attention first, if you don't mind."

Lina's husky laugh heated him from the inside out. "Of course."

He felt on top of the world. Reluctant to completely let go of her, he took her hand and led her toward the enclosure.

Then stopped in his tracks for the second time that day.

Betty had slipped right back into her earlier mood, all traces of the cheeky show-off vanished. His heart sank anew. She'd all but landed the job, and he couldn't stand to see her like this.

"What the hell?" he whispered. "She was brilliant when they were here."

Lina squeezed his hand in response, and together they approached the sad leopard.

"Betty, honey." He dropped Lina's hand and reached in to rub Betty's back. "What happened? We should be celebrating. Just pass your screen test, and you've got the job, doll. You did it."

She blinked up at him, huffed once, and then returned to her sulking.

Tony turned back to Lina. "I don't get it. She was on fire. And now…"

Lina shrugged, her tone oddly nervous. "I suppose she's an even better actor than you thought."

He grunted his assent. "But what do I do in the meantime? And will she be able to snap out of it again for the screen test?"

"So that's the next step?"

"Oh, yeah." He shook his head, trying to recapture some of his excitement. "The studio's filming something at a ranch nearby, so they thought it would be good to piggyback on that and do the test there. They're gonna call you about joining us for it."

"That's perfect." Lina's smile dazzled him.

He nodded. "It's good you'll be there. If she needs cheering up again."

A strange expression passed across her face. "Right."

"What did you say, anyway?" He waved his hand. "Hell, it doesn't even matter. Whatever it was, it worked, at least for a little while anyway."

Betty shifted behind him, and he faced her again, trying to infuse his voice with warmth rather than worry. "You've gotta snap out of this, girl. This is cause for a party. More treats."

He went to reach for her pail, only to find that it wasn't as near as he'd thought. What with his roller coaster of emotions, he hadn't noticed that Betty had moved over to the corner of the enclosure where they'd kept Bob before his release. The *closed* corner.

"Huh."

"What is it?" Lina asked.

"Nothing, it's only…" He pointed to Betty. "How in the world did she get in there?"

Lina chuckled. "Her enclosure?"

"No, *that* part of it." He stepped closer, peering to examine the inner fence, its gate currently ajar. "I could've sworn I left that latched."

"Maybe you left it open when you … cleaned it, or something?"

"I didn't go near it this morning. I was too concerned about Betty's mood."

"She probably pushed it open herself, then."

"Not possible. The latch is far too complicated," he muttered. *What the hell?* An odd tingle crept down his spine. According to Carl, Bob's circus jerks hadn't paid Betty any attention when they'd been there, but still...

He turned back to Lina. "You didn't see anything, or anyone, unusual back here, did you?"

"Me? No." She shook her head for emphasis, her dark waves swishing over her shoulders. "Maybe Gouda's developed a new talent?"

"Oh, god, don't even joke about that." *Shit.* Come to think of it, where was the kitten?

He heard a faint, tinny scratching sound and looked toward the house. He squinted at the kitchen window and sure enough, as if she'd somehow heard them, Gouda perched on the sill inside, framed perfectly through one of the windowpanes. She clawed at the glass a few more times before getting distracted by her own paw, which she began licking furiously.

Worry over the kitten settled at least, Tony rubbed at the back of his neck. Plenty of other fears mounted to take its place. The more he thought about Circus Jerk-us, the worse he felt.

"You're sure you didn't notice anything?" he asked Lina again.

"Like what?"

"Like two thugs from the circus..." He ran a hand through his hair and began pacing. "I wasn't here when they picked up Bob, but I wouldn't put it past them to get greedy. If anything happened to Betty..." He froze, then whirled back around to Lina. "Or you! Aw, hell. If they were nosing around here, they might've hurt you. Even the thought of my gals in danger..." He shuddered.

Lina's face softened. "Tony, relax. No one else was here." Her smile wobbled for a split second. "Just me."

He nodded, her reassurance working to some extent. But if his suspicions were incorrect... "That still doesn't explain how Betty got in there. I don't understand."

Something was definitely off, but the truth hovered frustratingly out of reach. It didn't help that Lina suddenly swallowed hard, her smile faltering again before turning too-bright altogether. As if she knew something she wasn't telling him.

"Lina, is something going on?"

"I beg your pardon?"

His words came out haltingly, fractured by his growing sense of unease. "First Betty's acting weird … and then not … and then weird again. And for a minute I thought she looked… Then I find her in a place she shouldn't be. And…"

He took in Lina's wide, worried eyes, and his shoulders sagged.

"I'm sorry. I think the stress is just getting to me." He pinched the bridge of his nose. "It's ridiculous, and impossible."

"What is?"

He raised his eyes back to hers with a mirthless chuckle. "I was this close to thinking you somehow hid Betty and smuggled another leopard in here to take her place for the audition." Before she could interject to tell him what a fool he was, he groaned. "I know. Maybe I just need a giant nap."

"Probably." She let out a weak laugh. "As if I could sneak a whole wild animal in here."

Tony exhaled. "You're about to run for the hills, aren't you?"

Her lips curved into a more genuine smile. "Of course not. You've been so anxious over all this. I understand."

She reached up to cup his cheek, and he melted into her touch, his eyes drifting closed for a moment. When his lids fluttered open again, though, his gaze caught on her blouse…

"Lina. Your buttons are off."

"What?"

He pointed as she glanced down at herself. "Your blouse. It's buttoned wrong."

Her finger, trembling slightly, rubbed at the top fastening. "Guess I was in such a hurry to get here this morning, I wasn't paying attention."

Tony shook his head. "No. It looked fine earlier. I would have noticed."

She attempted a haughty look—rather unsuccessfully. "Are you admitting you were staring at my tits, Tony?"

"Well, yeah. They're great tits," he admitted without reservation. "But you're trying to distract me. Why are your buttons wrong now?"

His brain was still struggling to catch that elusive ... whatever it was. Damned if he could figure it out.

He snorted as another absurd idea occurred to him. "Don't tell me. You donned a leopard suit and took Betty's place yourself?" he joked.

Her eyes widened briefly, before she narrowed them on him. "I guess I should be relieved you didn't accuse me of slipping off somewhere for an affair."

Guilt sent his stomach plummeting. "Oh, god. No. Of course I didn't think *that*." He hung his head. "I'm sorry, Lina. I really am a mess, aren't I?"

"No. You're not a mess." Her breath came out in a resigned sigh. "You're also ... not entirely wrong."

He stared at her in confusion, watching as she waged some sort of internal battle. Finally, she nodded, inhaled deeply, and squared her shoulders.

"It wasn't Betty who performed that audition with you. It was me."

Chapter Nine

Tony sputtered a laugh. "Are you trying to cheer me up with a joke?"

"No, I'm perfectly serious."

"Lina, I know there's no way you put on a leopard suit. First of all, even Opal and her counterparts in Wardrobe couldn't make one *that* believable. Granted, I was in such a state I could have been seeing things ... but Nick and the others weren't..."

He was rambling, he knew, but that weird tingle skittered over his spine again, and some instinct told him to keep talking so he didn't find out why. "Or wait. Did you mean the other thing? *Did you bring another cat to the audition? But that wouldn't explain your blouse.*"

"Tony." Her tone was sharp, and her eyes sparked a brighter gold than usual. An awfully familiar gold, come to think of it. It reminded him of those moments during Betty's audition, when... *No.* It wasn't the same.

"Would you please stop talking for a second and let me explain?" Her voice remained stern, but Lina's fingers beat out a staccato rhythm against her leg.

That nervous action shut his mouth, while doing nothing

whatsoever to quell his mounting sense that his world was about to get turned upside down. He managed a nod.

"Right." Lina took a deep breath. "So, I don't usually tell … anybody about this. Because of how it sounds, and because … well, there's the trust element." She blinked a few times in rapid succession. "But I do trust you. And you're so worried, and so sweet, about Betty and about potential danger, and… And you have a right to know, given everything." She gestured absently at Betty, before fixing her wide, golden eyes on him.

He didn't dare breathe.

"Tony, I have the ability to…" She squeezed her eyes shut, as if bracing for impact, her next words tumbling out in a rush. "I can change into a leopard at will, and that's what I did while the guys were here so it was me who did the audition with you, not Betty." She reopened one eye and squinted up at him with a grimace.

Tony stared at her. He wasn't entirely sure he remembered how to blink. He knew she waited for a response of some kind, but he remained frozen. Attempting to rearrange her words into an order that made any sort of sense.

He didn't succeed.

A few times, he tried speaking. When he finally managed more than incoherent sounds, he pushed out a single, "What?"

Seemingly relieved he hadn't keeled right over, Lina's face relaxed slightly. "I know how it sounds."

"Do you?" he croaked.

"Of course I do. Anyway. I wasn't having much luck with Betty, and time was running out, and I knew what I could do, so…" She lifted one shoulder. "I did it. I led Betty over there, transformed myself, and then when you all left, I switched back."

She said it as if it was that simple, and he supposed it would be—if it wasn't the most preposterous thing he'd ever heard.

But the eyes…

And the flirting…

Tony swallowed hard. "Lina, that's…"

"Unbelievable?"

"Yes." *Thank you.*

"Unheard of?"

"Yes."

"Utterly ridiculous?"

"Yeah."

She nodded. "You're right, it should be. But I assure you, it's not."

A strangled laugh escaped him as his rational mind fought against the gnawing sensation in his gut, and he feared she might be telling the truth. He mentally grasped for a lifeline, *any* lifeline…

"Okay, assuming all this is even possible, what about Betty, hmm?" He ignored the high pitch of his voice. "I was right here." He swept an arm in Betty's direction. "And she *wasn't there.*"

He nearly crowed in triumph when Lina crossed her arms over her chest and darted her eyes to the side.

Until she opened her mouth.

"As a complement to my shifting abilities, I have at my disposal a certain amount of … magic. Including the power of illusion. I glamoured that corner of the pen so that Betty would be undetectable to the regular human eye. All you might have noticed was a quick flash or a shimmer."

"What, like Dracula?" That opened up a horrific new can of worms. "Oh my god, are you saying you're a vampire too?"

"Don't be ridiculous. Vampires aren't real."

He cocked his head and shot her a disbelieving stare.

"Oh, don't look at me like that. Jaysus."

If her Irish accent was making an appearance, she must truly be agitated with him. But the sentiment was a two-way street.

"Why shouldn't I? You're asking me to believe that *Cat People* is real!" He threw up his hands. "Next thing I know, you're going to say we unlocked some kind of … sex magic the other day!"

Lina simply rolled her eyes.

He paused. "Did we…?" He glanced up at his bedroom

window, before dismissing the thought. "You know what, never mind. I don't want to know."

"Too bad. I'm going to tell you anyway." She arched one perfect eyebrow at his surprised look. "I hate to disappoint you, but *Cat People* was a work of rather sensationalized fiction, not a nature documentary. Sex has nothing whatsoever to do with this." Her face flushed, but she continued on. "I was magical long before *you* came along."

Her haughty attitude put him in his place—and okay, maybe he deserved it. But she punctuated her speech with a quick glance at his crotch that she couldn't seem to help, and paired with the still-deepening color in her cheeks, it told him plenty.

"Look, Lina." He pinched the bridge of his nose. "I don't know if you're having a go at me, or trying to distract me from worrying about Betty, or what. But this clearly isn't getting us anywhere. I—"

She cut him off with a world-weary sigh. "You're not going to believe me until you see it for yourself, are you?" she asked softly.

He wasn't sure if he was supposed to reply—not that she gave him the chance anyway. After darting a glance around the property, Lina bent her head and began unbuttoning her mis-buttoned blouse. Tony watched, slightly stunned, as she proceeded to remove all of her clothes and toss them on a nearby bench. When she'd finished, she stood before him, utterly beautiful, and held his gaze. Defiance—and trepidation—in her eyes.

He'd barely taken a full breath when the air ... shivered around her, and every hair on his body stood up. One blink, and Lina was gone. A gorgeous leopard stood in her place.

Tony staggered back as if punched.

He continued to stare while his mind frantically scrambled and stuttered. But the more he stared...

The spots, they were the same. His mind hadn't been playing tricks on him during the audition after all. And the eyes...

No wonder I thought of her.

It felt as if someone was sitting on his chest.

Wanting to make sense of something, anything, he looked to the corner of the enclosure. To Betty. She'd raised her head off her paws, but was otherwise unruffled at Lina's transformation. Tony glanced back and forth once more, and this time Betty looked him right in the eye, with an unnerving expression of amusement and impatience. As if to say, "She *did* tell you."

Deep down, some part of him had recognized the truth of what she told him. But that still didn't make it make sense. And he needed it to make sense…

By the time he turned his attention away from Betty, Lina was Lina again. He distantly registered all of her glorious skin and glorious curves, wishing he could focus on them instead.

She re-dressed quickly, and finally turned to face him. "Are you okay?"

Through the tumble of his roiling emotions, honesty won out. "No. I don't think I am." He blinked at her. "Lina…"

"I know."

Tony shook his head. "I'm not sure you do." His thoughts were engaged in a full-on wrestling match at this point, and the lonely coffee he'd consumed for breakfast churned painfully in his stomach. Of their own volition, his legs started pacing, his steps halting and jerky. "I don't… I can't… How…?"

He rubbed his temples, desperation mounting for *one* thing to ground him amid the chaos of what was, apparently, now possible in the world. When he caught sight of Betty, a familiar worry popped into his head, and he seized on it.

Tony stilled. "Lina, what did you do?"

"What?"

The swirling storm coalesced around that single kernel, and he pivoted to face her.

"The audition. What did you do?" he repeated.

"I … helped?"

He hated how small her voice sounded, but he didn't think he could let go of this now. "No. No, you didn't. Not really. Maybe for a few minutes, but… What the hell am I going to do now?"

"I beg your pardon?"

"You took Betty's place."

"And I nailed it!"

"Yeah, but look at her." He waved at the leopard. "She's still not herself. I have absolutely no idea how to fix her. She's in no shape to perform. But thanks to you, hamming it up, she's going to have to! In just a few days!"

Lina let out an affronted huff at his critique of her performance, and it should have given him pause. But he was powerless to stop the onslaught at this point, and so on he rolled.

"What the hell happens when I can't snap her out of it, and the screen test arrives anyway?" She opened her mouth to answer, but he cut her off. "And don't say you can do this again. Because you can't. You have to act alongside her, remember?"

"Oh."

"That's right. *Oh.* You can't pull some Superman-Clark Kent trick, never being seen in the same place together, and miraculously no one notices. The whole point of all this is for you two to be on screen, at the same time!"

"I didn't think—"

"No! You didn't think! You jumped right in, consequences be damned, and thought it would be a good idea to *be* my leopard!"

Hurt flashed in Lina's eyes, and somewhere in the recesses of his mind, his *heart*, Tony regretted his tirade. But if he loosened his grip on his anger, even a little, he'd start thinking about the fact that his new girlfriend had just transformed into a fucking leopard, right before his eyes, and how was that even possible, that magic was real and—

Screen test. Betty. Screen test. Betty.

"In only a couple of days, in front of a whole hell of a lot of people—yourself included—I have to deliver a fully functioning leopard. One who can now apparently do even bigger and better tricks than I trained her to do. Thanks to you."

Lina's nostrils flared with each rapid breath she took. Worse, anger had eclipsed the hurt, turning her eyes more luminous—and mutinous.

"At least I was doing something other than pace and panic," she hissed.

He wanted to protest, but words eluded him, now that his momentum had slowed.

She pounced on his hesitation, stepping closer to him. "I am sorry if you think I made things worse. That was not my intention. I thought we could figure out whatever the next step is *together*."

He flinched at that, a weight sinking in his stomach.

"Clearly I thought wrong," Lina added in a near-whisper, before raising her voice once again and poking a finger in the center of his chest. "But I did buy you some fucking time. Which you might realize when you get your head out of your ass." She punctuated this with another jab, even more painful this time.

She whirled on her heel and stalked away. Too late to capture her hand, pull her close, and take it all back, Tony instead rubbed at the spot on his chest that hurt both inside and out.

Lina was nearly to the stables when she called over her shoulder, "Good luck with this one, Betty."

She disappeared around the building, leaving him to stare blankly after her. The faint rumble of her car triggered the avalanche he'd been holding at bay, and everything about the last hour crashed down on him. He stumbled back a few steps and sank onto the bench outside Betty's enclosure.

Lina had leapt in to help where he couldn't ... and had gotten Betty closer to a part that could secure their future ... because she could *transform herself* into a fucking *leopard*. Because *magic* was apparently real. And he...

"Ohhhh, I am an asshole."

At his side, Betty huffed her clear agreement, and he buried his face in his hands with a groan.

Chapter Ten

Lina stared, unseeing, at her script pages, the words swimming hazily in front of her. She had a bit of time before they needed her in Makeup, so she waited in her dressing room and sought to distract herself by going over her lines.

No such luck.

The entire bloody debacle with Tony had been replaying on a continuous loop in her mind since she'd left the sanctuary the day before. All afternoon, all night, all this morning—over and over, it haunted her. Made her alternately angry and mopey … not to mention hot and bothered.

She groaned. That might be the worst part. She wanted to stay furious, but every once in a while, the audition itself popped into her memory—specifically, Tony's commands in that lovely, deep voice of his—and heat built all over again, started her squirming…

NO. He does not deserve your hot and bothered.

Lina threw the script pages on her dressing table and massaged her temples. She had no idea what she'd been thinking. Yes, she'd helped Betty; she didn't regret that part. But the aftermath, *trusting* Tony? That was another story entirely.

True, she had dropped quite a bombshell on him. One he clearly wasn't prepared to comprehend. But did he need to be quite that much of a jackass about it?

She switched the cross of her legs and fiddled with her ring, the stone warm against her fingers. What she wanted, more than anything, was to talk to Alice. In her official position, she'd likely admonish Lina for sharing her secret, and perhaps for using her powers to intervene in the audition in the first place. If Lina was being honest, it was exactly the kind of impulsive behavior that would have—and often *had*—gotten her in trouble with her elders in her youth. Perhaps Tony had hit more of a nerve than he even realized.

Lina inhaled deeply, pushing the thought away, and instead refocused on Alice. All business aside, as Lina's friend she'd be able to commiserate, help her make sense of everything—good and bad—she felt for Tony at the moment. At the very least, she could give Lina a hug.

Lina really wanted a hug.

But Alice was miles away, not easily reachable by telephone. And this wasn't enough of an emergency to justify using her ring to put out a distress call. Despite how distressing this situation felt to her.

A soft knock on her dressing room door pulled her out of her bubble. She hadn't expected her Makeup call so soon. Ready for the distraction, she waited for a voice to confirm, but none followed. That was odd; typically, the production assistants spoke up before she got to the door. When a second knock sounded, she rose from her chair, tightening the sash on her robe as she walked. She opened the door to find—

"Oh. It's you."

Tony stood at the foot of the trailer's two steps, putting him just below her eye level. He looked … a mess. *Well, that's something.*

The waves of his hair were barely tamed into submission. He wore a tie, its knot nowhere near successful, and decidedly off-center. Dark circles hovered beneath his eyes, as if he'd gotten a terrible night's sleep, if he'd slept at all. He clutched a parcel wrapped in brown paper and colorful twine, hopelessly smushed under his hand.

Lina was pretty hopeless herself—torn between thinking he painted an oddly adorable picture, and wanting to grab the package and bash him over the head with it.

She hadn't made up her mind yet when he spoke, his voice rough. "Could we..." He cleared his throat. "Do you think we could talk? I know I'm probably the last person you want to see right now, but..."

He wasn't too far off-base, but his remorse was obvious. Since he'd gotten his head at least part of the way out of his ass, she stood back to let him in. And if his cedar-like scent sent a shot of warmth gliding down her spine, she sure as hell didn't have to admit that to him.

Instead, she closed the door, shutting them into the small space. As relieved as she was to see him apologetic, and with a gift no less, she didn't know what he was going to say. Or just how much—and what in particular—he regretted about the scene yesterday.

Lina folded her arms across her chest. "I'm expected in Makeup soon, so I don't have a ton of time."

"Right. Of course. I won't keep you." He took a deep breath, but didn't say more.

She pointed to the parcel. "Is that for me?"

"Yes! I... Oh." He lifted it and caught sight of the way he'd mangled it, his face falling. "Sorry, it looked much better before, I swear." He held up his offering, and she accepted gingerly.

Its slightly hefty weight surprised her, as did its odd scent. If she didn't know better, she'd say it smelled like...

"Is this ... *meat*?"

Tony's face flushed crimson as his words tumbled over one another. "I actually thought about getting you catnip, but I wasn't sure if you went in for that sort of thing. But then I remembered what you brought Betty, and talking about expensive tastes and all, and so … filet mignon!" He punctuated the reveal with a sad little flourish of his hands in the direction of the package.

She split a stunned glance between him and the … *filet mignon* she held. But he wasn't finished.

"I was all set to invite you over and make it for you, but then I had no idea if you like medium rare, or well done, or… So I just…" He paused, his breath audibly hitching. He raised horrified eyes to hers. "Oh my god. I brought you raw meat. To your trailer."

Despite her surprise, Lina fought the urge to laugh. "Thank you?"

He groaned. "What was I thinking? I've fucked this up even more, haven't I?"

It was rather a sweet gesture, however horrifically misguided. She decided to take a little pity on him. "You haven't. Not entirely. But maybe next time, stick to chocolate or flowers."

Tony huffed a shocked laugh, whether at her tone or her use of the words *next time*, she wasn't sure. She'd surprised herself a bit with that, too.

"Will do," he said. "Look, I know I'm terrible in my execution, but I wanted to do *something*, and…" He let out a giant sigh. "Let me start over."

Lina watched as he inhaled once more, squared his shoulders, then met her eyes directly. The intensity she saw in the deep brown of his gaze hit her right in the heart.

"Lina, I am so sorry. The way I handled everything yesterday was atrocious. I wouldn't blame you if you never wanted to see me again. But I had to at least come and explain." He reached up, but caught himself before running his hand through his hair, quickly dropping his arm again. "Betty, and the sanctuary, are everything to me. I want the world for her, and sometimes, more often than I should, I let my worries get the better of me. Yesterday, I was already up to a million, and then … you…" He gestured vaguely in her direction. "I know you were trying to help, but my brain just shut down. And left nothing but an asshole in its wake.

"Not that it excuses my behavior," he rushed on. "What you said yesterday, about not sharing this with people… And then I turned around and proved exactly why that's a wise choice." He shook his head, slow and sad. "You trusted me with a side of you no one gets to see. And I dishonored that trust. I am so sorry."

Lina swallowed against the lump in her throat, tears threatening. "Thank you." She toyed with the wilted twine on her gift. "And yes, you did behave like rather a shit."

He let out a strangled sound, a mix of startled and amused. "That's fair," he rasped.

"But I did deliver you quite a shock," she admitted, allowing herself a half smile.

"*That's* an understatement."

Seeing as she'd never confessed her biggest secret to anyone before, Lina wasn't sure what to say next. Tony's apology was heartfelt, and he likely had a ton of questions for her. But even though she'd technically started all of this, she debated her readiness to actually answer them. An awkward silence descended, during which she belatedly realized she still held a package of raw meat. Gently, she set it on her dressing table.

Turning back to face him, Lina considered making another joke about the gift. But something in Tony's expression gave her pause. He regarded her with a combination of wonder and something else, almost like anticipation. *That's odd.*

"Sorry," she began, "I'm at a bit of a loss for words."

"Oh … right." Now he looked … disappointed.

She watched him for a moment, slowly realizing that, behind it all, a hint of defensiveness crept into his features. As though…

An awful suspicion dawned, and she narrowed her eyes. "Wait a moment. Are you… You're not expecting *me* to apologize too, are you?"

"No!" He bit his lip. "Well … maybe. A little."

Lina opened her mouth to protest, but all that emerged was an indignant, incoherent noise.

Running a hand through his hair, Tony barreled on. "Look, that wasn't my intention in coming here, I swear. I really did just want to make up for *my* reaction."

Willing herself to remain calm, haughty even, she arched an eyebrow. "But...?"

"But... Yeah, now that I'm here, an apology would be nice to hear." He held up a hand. "I meant every word I said, Lina. I didn't handle anything well yesterday, and I am sorry for it. But the fact remains..." He sighed. "You may have bought us a little more time, but you also put me, and Betty, in a really awkward position. It was impulsive, and reckless, and I have no idea how to fix it if I can't get her to perform."

His words stung. She wasn't ignorant of the hurt lurking underneath them, but her own hurt rose higher. That nerve she'd suspected he hit was now a live wire under her skin. *Impulsive. Reckless.* She'd heard it before. Worked hard to curb not only her reaction to it, but the behavior itself.

Yet here she was, all over again. And with this man who inspired feelings she hadn't even begun to sort through.

She swallowed it down, and leaned into her own defensiveness. "I told you yesterday, I was simply trying to help where you couldn't."

"I know. And you did. But Lina, can't you at least see where I'm coming from? The new problems I have to deal with now?"

Deep down, she could. She knew she could. But anger made her stubborn, even in the face of his handsome features, twisted in desperation to make her understand. Her magic sparked under her skin, no longer comforting or intriguing, but itchy with her agitation.

Lina closed her eyes and breathed deeply against the emotions she'd thought long-buried, emotions at war with her desire to fix everything and return them to where they'd been only the day before.

She heard Tony's weary exhale before he spoke. "I guess I made a mistake in coming here. I should let you go."

Whether he meant it casually, or in a more permanent sense, she couldn't tell. But before she could respond, a brisk knock at her door interrupted the moment.

"Telegram for you, Miss Leonard," a page's voice called out.

Lina quickly opened the door and accepted the offered envelope.

"Thank you," she told the page. "Do you know if they're ready for me in Makeup yet?"

The page's face scrunched in confusion. "Golly, I don't know. I could check for you."

She shook her head. "No, that's all right. I'm sure someone will be along soon. Thanks."

"Sure thing, Miss Leonard!"

Lina once again closed herself into the small space with Tony, though she couldn't bring herself to look at him, instead focusing on her telegram. Her throat tightened when she opened it.

Still lots of work to do up here. Stop. Will be at least a few more days. Stop. Hope all is quiet with you. Stop. Talk soon, Alice.

The fight left her, along with her breath. It was nothing unexpected, but getting this tangible confirmation that Alice remained inaccessible to her made her disappointment that much more acute. She sagged against the door.

"Is everything okay?" Tony asked softly.

She glanced up at him, the kind concern in his eyes nearly making her forget why they'd been arguing in the first place.

"Yes." Pointing to the telegram, she explained, "While my friend is away, I'm filling in for her. With regard to … cat-related things. She's just letting me know she'll be a little longer."

"Oh." He nodded as if he understood, despite the clear confusion on his face.

Suddenly, she didn't want him to try to leave again.

"I'm sorry, Tony." His eyes widened in surprise, but she raised the paper in her hand and continued, "This life—I knew pretty young that I wasn't cut out for it. In part because of my tendency to be…" She forced herself to meet his gaze directly, repeating his words back to him. "Impulsive. And reckless. I think that's part of the reason the elders didn't begrudge me going off on my own. They were rather relieved."

"Lina," he whispered. "I didn't know."

"You couldn't have."

"But still, I poked at a bruise."

"To be fair, my reaction surprised me a bit, too. I thought it didn't bother me as much as it used to anymore." She bit her lip. "And … you weren't wrong. All my stubbornness aside, I do see the difficult road you've got ahead of you, and I'm sorry for my contribution to it."

"Thank you."

The ensuing quiet this time was not comfortable, precisely, but no longer so fraught, at least. She wasn't sure where they went from here, with both of their apologies still raw as the meat he'd given her. Plus, there still remained the million questions he must have for her.

Thinking it best to let them both catch their breath, she moved to her dressing table and laid the telegram next to Tony's gift, which made her smile more genuinely.

She turned back around to find that Tony had clearly not caught his breath, his face instead taking on much of the same shock he'd displayed when she revealed herself the day before. He blinked at her, eyes wide and a little wild. But also now … impressed?

"So … you're a leopard," he breathed.

Chapter Eleven

Right. Here come those questions. Lina blushed, very much against her will.

Her nerves brought out her pedantic side. "I'm not, actually. I am a human being with the magical ability to transform my shape into that of a leopard. But I'm still very much me when I do."

"Right. Yeah. Okay." He shoved his hands in his pockets, looking dazed, but his voice filled with awe. "There are so many things I want to ask you, but I don't think I have the right to."

"You do," she replied quietly.

He raised hopeful eyes to hers, and when she nodded her confirmation, his lips quirked into a lopsided smile that was too damn endearing.

She gestured at her couch. "Come on, why don't we sit."

He followed her over, and she immediately questioned the wisdom of her idea. Not because it was unpleasant—just the opposite. Being in such close proximity to him, his scent and his heat encroaching on her, made it nearly impossible to resist touching him. But it was crucial she keep her wits about her, if she was going to give him the answers they both needed in order to determine what came next.

She folded her hands primly in her lap. "Is there anything particular you want to ask first, or…?"

Tony opened his mouth, closed it, and then repeated the process a few times before finally giving up with a groan. "I honestly don't even know. I have so many. I can't believe something like this, someone like you, is even possible."

"Sometimes I wonder a bit, myself." At his low chuckle, she smiled, more fully than she had since he arrived, and it gave her a boost of courage. "Would it help if I just told you a bit about myself, and my people?"

"Sure." He paused, before his next words rushed out. "But please don't feel you have to tell me anything. I'll completely understand if there are things I shouldn't know. And of course, you have my word that I'll keep all of this to myself."

"I appreciate that. Thank you. There is plenty I can tell you, though. We don't spread it around, obviously, but it's not as if we're sworn to some secrecy pact punishable by exile, or anything, either."

"That's a relief."

Lina huffed a laugh. "It is. And we stay undetected largely because most people simply wouldn't imagine we exist. Like you."

He nodded, and she took a moment to gather her thoughts. *Where to begin…?*

"So," she began, perhaps a little too formally, "I come from a long line of people, women mostly, gifted centuries ago with certain abilities. For the primary purpose of protecting the world's feline population, of all shapes and sizes."

"Something we have in common, then," he interjected softly. "I mean, I can't do anything nearly as nifty as you, but…"

Lina nodded, feeling her shoulders relax. "True. But the intentions are the same. Anyway, our main gift is being able to transform ourselves, but we also have varying degrees of supplemental magic at our disposal."

"Like the illusion you created yesterday."

"Mm-hmm. It's useful for avoiding detection, obviously. But even more important, we can also … project things to the cats under our care, to help them with healing and comfort and the like. It's mostly just energy; we can't magically make an injury disappear or anything. Unfortunately. But it's something."

"And it's only cats?"

"Only cats. Not that we don't appreciate other creatures. But the cats are our responsibility, our birthright."

"You said you'd been gifted with it… Am I allowed to ask by who? You're originally from Ireland, right? Is it something to do with the Druids? I don't know much about them, but … I've at least heard hints of their mythology."

She warmed further at his curiosity. "Yes. To it all. You're allowed to ask, *and* we can trace our roots to some Celtic goddesses."

"Wow." He took a long inhale. "That must be really hard for you to balance, huh? Is it like having a whole second career, beyond your acting? Or wait, what you said earlier … about being on your own…?" He grimaced. "I'm sorry. You probably don't want to talk about it."

"It's okay." Lina paused. "Just, um…"

He nodded in understanding, giving her a moment. She was rather touched by his concern, not only for the difficulty of the subject, but simply for her life in general, her well-being. She swallowed.

"You're right, it would be a balancing act. If I'd fully committed to that life." Despite hinting at it over Alice's telegram, Lina hadn't planned on going into too much detail about this aspect of her story when she'd moved on to answering his questions. Old, familiar guilt flared, pressing on that nerve all over again.

But Tony's empathy surrounded her now like a warm blanket, prompting her to want to try explaining the rest.

He might as well know it all.

"We have a choice, you see. When we're younger and our powers start to manifest, we go through a lot of training. And in the end, it's ultimately up to each of us whether we keep going with it." She risked a glance at him, but he regarded her with only kind curiosity.

"And you decided not to?" he asked quietly.

She shook her head. He reached out to tentatively brush his fingers against the back of her hand. Needing it more than she'd realized, she flipped her hand over and laced their fingers together.

"I knew from a pretty early age that my future lay elsewhere. In part because of my impetuous streak."

He grimaced, then squeezed her hand.

She returned the gesture before continuing, "But also… We see a lot of suffering, you know? The thought of taking all that on, of getting my heart broken over and over and over… I didn't think I could do it. I realize how selfish that sounds, but I swear it's not, not entirely. You need a certain detachment, when you're helping them. To get through it and actually help. I never could detach, not really." She finished with a small shrug.

Tony cradled her hand between both of his. "Hey, I understand that. It's why Carl is the vet and I'm the trainer-slash-therapy guy. You've seen how I get." His mouth kicked up into his lopsided smile.

Relief—chased by something more magical—shot through her. "That I have. But I still feel guilty sometimes."

"You said it's a choice, though. Did your family, any of your people, make you feel bad for it?" A protective undertone threaded through his voice, rather gratifyingly.

"No, actually. Which makes me feel *more* guilty, for some stupid reason." She let out a rueful laugh. "Maybe if they'd pushed back a little more, I'd feel more defiant than chagrined. But they understood. I think plenty of the elders were disappointed. My powers have always been pretty strong, even when latent."

"So you're impressive in many ways."

"Damn right." Her cheeks flushed, but she no longer minded. "But as strong as my magic is, everyone's always said my spirit is even stronger."

He cleared his throat. "Hence the nerve I hit."

Lina huffed a laugh, surprising herself. Clearing the air with Tony was proving oddly cathartic. "Exactly. As much as they admired my skills, I suspect they were a wee bit relieved to see *me* go." His expression darkened, and she shook her head. "Not that anyone was harsh about it. And when I'm not caught off guard, I can actually admit that it's … something I needed to work on. Still do, I suppose."

Tony's soft grin eased her spirits. "And I suppose I could do with a little less panicking."

"We're both works in progress." She exhaled fully for the first time all day, and judging by his expression, he felt the same. They were finally back where they'd been headed before the audition.

After a beat, she continued, "Anyway. I didn't meet with a lot of resistance when I left home. On top of all the rest, since I knew early on I wasn't going into protection, I never quite took my training seriously enough."

"Now we're getting to the good stuff." He shifted on the couch to face her, his dark eyes alight with anticipation.

She playfully swatted him on the shoulder. "Oh, stop it. I wasn't that bad. Hardly salacious."

He let out a grunt of mock disappointment, before growing serious. "All kidding aside, I am glad you come from a place where you had the grace to make your own way in the world. And not just because it brought you here to Hollywood."

Her breath caught. "Me too."

Tony brushed her hair behind her ear, his fingers lingering to caress her cheek. Lina's eyes drifted closed, and she let herself bask in the warmth of his touch.

"Can I ask you something else?" His voice was a delicious, deep whisper.

Without opening her eyes, she replied, "You can."

"When you shift..." His thumb traced a lazy circle over her skin. "Can you make yourself any cat, or is it only a leopard? I don't think they're native to Ireland."

Lina snickered. "They are not. And no." She opened her eyes to find him staring fixedly at her lips, and suppressed a shiver. "None of us can change into multiple cats, just one each. Another of our choices. Once our powers start manifesting, we're supposed to study all the fiercer felines, and when we come of age, pick the one we want to transform into. Based on everything we've learned."

"And you chose a leopard, of all cats." The hushed wonder in his voice sounded simultaneously thrilling and nerve-wracking.

"Mm-hmm."

His eyebrows quirked up. "Why do I sense a story there?"

Lina bit her lip. "Let's just say, my decision to pick a leopard had less to do with studied knowledge than my coven mates'."

He watched her for a moment, waiting for her to elaborate. When she didn't, he prodded, "You're not just going to leave me hanging like that, are you?"

Aw, hell. In for a penny...

"I may have chosen the great and majestic leopard primarily because..." She squeezed her eyes shut. "...I liked the print."

A charged silence followed, where she debated slinking off the couch and escaping to the Makeup room. But then—oh, then—Tony erupted into laughter. It was deep, and hearty, and *perfect*. She joined him in the glorious release. Any lingering hints of tension between them evaporated.

Her heart felt free again, even more so now, because he knew. There was plenty they still needed to talk about, unanswered questions about her past and their future, and what to do about Betty. But they'd begun to clear the air. More importantly, he knew the truth of her, and he hadn't run screaming back to the hills.

When their laughter began to ebb, she couldn't help herself. She closed the distance between them and pressed her lips to his. His curved up in response, before they melted into each other. Relief and desire mingled, along with a hot, satisfying spark of her magic. As if it recognized something in Tony. She'd shied away from her power for so long, but it felt welcome once more.

They broke apart for air, and rested their foreheads together with twin sighs.

"You don't use your gifts very much at all," Tony began, before hesitating. "But you did for Betty."

"And for you," she replied quietly.

Tony's exhale ghosted over her skin. "And look what I did with that."

"I didn't think past the audition. Then I sent you into shock." She reached up to push a stray auburn wave off his forehead. "But you're here now."

"And I plan to earn my way back to staying." His soft, steely promise sent a warm shiver down her spine. He held her gaze as he continued, "Thank you. For trying to help us both."

"How is Betty today? Any improvement?"

Tony's face fell, and he shook his head defeatedly. "She's less lethargic, I guess, but still awfully mopey."

"I'm sure we can figure out how to help her."

His eyes brightened. "*We?*"

Lina's lips curved upward. "We. Assuming you want my help, I'd still like to do all I can to help you and Betty."

"Are you kidding? Of course I do. I am so sorry I ever let you believe otherwise." He gave her a tentative smile of his own as his fingers brushed over her cheek. "You really think we can raise her spirits in time for the screen test?"

"I do. Just watch, I'll make an optimist out of you yet, Tony Benson."

His laugh was a low rumble. "Patron saint of lost causes, are you?"

He didn't give her a chance to come up with a witty retort

before his lips found hers again. They both moaned at the contact, and it didn't take long for their soft, gentle nips at each other to deepen. Their passionate spark ignited, her fingers tangled in his hair while he grasped her waist tightly, the heat of his touch searing her through the thin silk of her robe.

Tony peppered a trail of open-mouthed kissed over her jaw and down her throat. Lina took his earlobe in a gentle bite, reveling in his hiss of pleasure. When his hand slithered further down, grazing her ass, she pressed herself into him, unable to get close enough. She swung her leg up and slithered into his lap, straddling him.

He groaned, in what sounded like relief and agony both, as she settled against his already hardening cock. They fit together so well; she'd be more than content to sit on any part of him, anytime. Lina smiled against his lips, and felt his answering grin, before sliding her tongue along his. She wrapped her arms fully around his neck, and he took a more generous handful of her ass while his other hand slid scorchingly up her back, making her arch into his touch.

Tony pulled his mouth from hers with a chuckle. "Are you actually purring?"

She leaned back and arched an eyebrow at him. "Would that be a problem if I was?"

One side of his mouth quirked upward. "Hell no."

She'd mostly been teasing him, but it was still nice to hear. "Good."

Their lips had barely made contact again when a sharp, loud knock at her door jolted them apart.

A production assistant's voice followed. "They're ready for you in Makeup, Miss Leonard."

"Oh, um, right. I'll be along in a minute," she called back. She remembered to tack on a last-second thanks, before meeting Tony's wild, dazed look.

"I forgot you're at work," he rasped.

"Honestly, so did I."

"Guess it's a good thing we did all this *before* you got your makeup done."

Lina snickered as she eased herself off his lap. "Very true. I do wish I didn't have to go." She risked a glance down at his poor, straining erection. "Are you all right if I leave you here with that situation in your trousers?"

He grunt-laughed. "I'll manage." He bit his lip rather adorably. "Though, would you mind if I linger in here until it gets a bit less … situational?"

"Of course. Stay as long as you need." She reached down to cup his cheek. "I'm really glad you came by today."

He turned his head and kissed her palm. "Me too."

"I'm on set pretty much all day, but I could come out to the sanctuary later for dinner and some strategizing. Among other things."

Tony took her hand in his with a gentle squeeze. "I would absolutely love that. All of it. And if the drive's too much, I can come to you."

"I don't mind. I'd like to say hi to Betty too."

"She'd like that." His expression grew sheepish. "Why don't I take your, um … gift back with me? I can cook it properly for you later."

"Perfect. Medium-well, by the way."

"Duly noted."

Lina reluctantly stepped away from him to give herself a once-over in the mirror. "Oh, hell, I'm a mess," she muttered, smoothing her disheveled hair.

"I think you look great." Tony's sly smile nearly drew her right back to his lap. "Besides, isn't that the whole point of where you're going?"

"In theory, yes, you smart aleck. But if I go over there looking like I've just been thoroughly ravished, it'll raise more questions than answers." Having achieved a sufficient degree of smoothing —despite the uncontainable flush on her cheeks—Lina gave his hair a little revenge ruffle on her way to the door. "I'll see you tonight."

"See you later. Break a leg in your scenes today."

"Thanks." She feathered one last kiss across his lips, day significantly improved. She headed over to Makeup, already counting down the minutes until she could pull Tony into her arms again.

Chapter Twelve

It was nearly sunset when Lina arrived at the sanctuary. She found Tony out back, gently rubbing Betty's back through the enclosure fence. Both man and beast looked up at her approach, setting off a mix of emotion within Lina. While it broke her heart to see Betty still so desolate, her pulse sped up considerably at the way Tony's face brightened.

"Hi," she greeted him.

"Hello." He took her hand and kissed it like a perfect gentleman, though the fire in his eyes was anything but courtly. He lowered his arm but didn't let her go.

She allowed herself—and him—a contented purr before turning to Betty.

"Hey, pretty lady." With her free hand, Lina gave the leopard a scratch behind the ears. "Still missing your fella?"

Betty let out a forlorn huff.

"You poor dear." Because she now could without reservation, she summoned her magic and sent a pulse of calming energy into Betty. As she did, she felt a tingle in the hand Tony still held. *Huh. That's new.* She'd analyze whatever it meant later—the important thing at the moment was the reassuring rumble emanating from

Betty. It might not be enough to get her up and doing tricks yet, but at least Lina was providing the cat some comfort.

Tony inhaled audibly and his fingers squeezed hers.

"You're doing something right now," he whispered.

Her focus on her task wavered as she answered him. "I am."

"I think … I can see it." His voice was low, astonished. "It's like a … a golden glow."

Lina stared at him for a moment before following his gaze to where her hand rested on Betty's head. "I always feel, and sometimes see, a spark, but I've often wondered if anyone outside our circle would be able to pick up on it. I've never tested the theory before."

The wonder on his face, as if he was humbled and honored, made her knees weak.

"I probably wouldn't have noticed, if I didn't know." His lips kicked up into a grin. "It's in your eyes, too. They … they shimmer." He trailed his finger over the top of her cheekbone. "So luminous. Beautiful."

She forgot how to breathe.

"Thank you," he said quietly. "For letting me see it."

Lina managed a nod, her voice having fled the scene along with her breath. But her body hadn't entirely shut down—her pulse beat, hot and steady, between her legs. *That* she could act on.

Unfortunately, Betty chose that moment to grunt, having noticed that Lina's hand had slid from its protective spot.

Lina drew back with a sharp breath. "We shouldn't."

"Right." Tony dropped both his hands, disappointment flashing across his face.

Said disappointment made her smile. She placed her hand over his heart, which was beating out a fast, and rather gratifying, rhythm.

"I only meant, not here." Lina nodded toward Betty. "Since she's feeling so lonely, it's hardly sporting of us to act all lovey-dovey right in front of her."

"That's true," he chuckled. Tony took in Betty with a resigned sigh, and held Lina's hand against his chest, while brushing his other over the leopard's back.

If Lina were painting their portrait, she'd title it *A Lad and His Two Best Gals.* She held in a laugh at the thought, and was glad she did when he spoke to Betty, still serious.

"Don't worry, girl. We'll figure out how to get you feeling better. I promise," he finished softly.

Lina swallowed around the lump in her throat, as Tony squared his shoulders and faced her again, smile back in place. And plenty of heat in his eyes—which sent her blood fizzing again.

"I set us up for dinner upstairs. Are you hungry?"

She shot him a seductive smirk. "Oh, I'm hungry, all right."

TONY QUICKLY DETOURED to grab the plates of steak and spaghetti he'd set in the oven to keep warm, before leading Lina upstairs to his loft. Her soft gasp when she reached the top of the stairs warmed him to his core.

"Tony. What is all this?"

He shrugged as much as he could without upending their food. "Our last dinner here was unforgivably casual. Besides, I wanted to do something nice, after everything yesterday…"

She'd forgiven him, but that didn't alleviate his guilt over his previous behavior.

He set their plates down on the table he'd arranged near his window seat. It was only a cheap card table, but he'd dressed it with the nicest tablecloth he had. He didn't own much in the way of candlesticks, but he'd found a scrap of ribbon at the back of a drawer and tied it around an empty wine bottle. He'd tried to capture the mood of an Italian restaurant, and hoped she found it charming rather than cheesy.

As Lina stepped up next to him, he held his breath. But she

cradled his face in both her hands and smiled so brightly it nearly knocked him on his ass.

"It's just perfect. Thank you."

His cheeks heated, but he didn't care. Lina was glorious, and she was here with him, and he'd do his level best to keep her.

Tony bent his head to kiss her, as he'd wanted to do out at the enclosure. He planned to take his time, linger over the way she tasted—mostly of mint, with an underlying hint of vanilla that he suspected came from her lipstick. But she opened immediately to him, licking into his mouth and igniting a fire that had him tightly gripping her waist.

When she wound her fingers into his hair with another of her distinct purring sounds, he couldn't help his chuckle. She arched her eyebrow in that way that was beginning to drive him as crazy as her hands in his hair.

"I'm sorry, it's only…" How to explain without sounding like he was making fun?

She grimaced, then narrowed her eyes in a clear attempt to cover her embarrassment. "I'm making cat sounds again, aren't I?"

Tony bit his lip and nodded. At her immediate blush, he rushed on, "But I swear, that's not a complaint. It's rather adorable." She opened her mouth to protest, but he stalled her with another kiss. "And sexy."

There's her saucy smile.

"Oh?"

"Yes." He punctuated his assurance with one more peck. "It's funny, all the things I noticed, but didn't… Until now."

"Now that you know."

He nodded. "Now that I know." He slid his arms loosely around her waist, appreciating the way hers relaxed over his shoulders.

Everything she'd revealed to him swirled strangely through his thoughts; there was a part of him that still couldn't quite believe what he'd seen with his own eyes. But overriding that was his growing awe that Lina had somehow chosen to trust *him* with all of it. All of *her*. He wanted to be worthy of that trust. Wanted to keep reassuring her.

"I should've told you sooner but … you gave quite an extraordinary performance yesterday."

"What, at the audition?"

"Mm-hmm. You were wonderful. All those little flourishes you added to the act…"

Her expression remained skeptical. "You mean the ones Betty won't be able to replicate?"

Tony winced. "I'm so sorry for the way I overreacted."

"You didn't. It's true, I got a little carried away."

"Even so, it worked. And maybe Betty can pick them up eventually. But I've been thinking, I'll have to teach her a bunch of new commands for the movie anyway. So we just need to get her through that screen test, make Nick and the others appreciate whatever she *can* do." He pulled her closer. "And I more than appreciate what you can do. What you did."

Lina's soft, almost shy smile made his stomach do all kinds of backflips.

"Betty is a quick study," she said. "With a little coaching, I'm sure I can impart some of my skills."

"I am too." He tucked a strand of hair behind her ear. "You know, you're a very talented actress, even in leopard form."

Her throaty laugh sounded like music. "Thank you, sir."

She bit her lip. Tony watched in fascination as she waged some internal debate. He desperately wanted to encourage her, but also feared pushing her too hard. He clocked the minute she registered her decision, but nearly lost all his mental capacity to process anything when her index finger began toying with the hair at the base of his neck.

"Who's purring now?" she asked with a smirk.

"Says the woman who looks like she just cornered a mouse."

Lina shrugged one elegant shoulder. "If the claw fits…"

They laughed together, before his impatience won out. "You were about to say something?"

A lovely hint of color crept into her cheeks. "I was. About yesterday, and the audition…? I have a bit of a confession to make."

"Another one?" Tony cocked his head to one side, curious this time.

She nodded. "You're pretty talented yourself, you know. All those instructions, those … commands…" Her throat worked on a swallow, and she raised hungry golden eyes to his. He nearly keeled over. "I liked them."

"You did?" he croaked.

"Quite a lot, actually." Her gaze darted briefly to his mouth. "As a matter of fact, it made me want to show off even more."

Pride and lust surged within him. "I've always believed the key to a good performance is plenty of reward."

Hungry intrigue dawned across her pretty features, her eyes practically glowing now.

Oh, the rewards I could give her… He went almost fully hard at the prospect, even as a memory hit him. "The treats I gave you ended up in a pile. Because it was *you*, and not Betty."

Her mouth curved in a rueful smile. "Noticed that, did you?"

Tony hummed his assent. He traced her bottom lip with one finger, then bent to whisper across her jaw. "I gave you the wrong reward, didn't I?" Her breath hitched satisfyingly when he reached her earlobe and gave it a gentle bite. "I'm going to have to fix that." He traced the shell of her ear with his tongue, setting her shivering—and purring again. "Reward you properly this time. Would you like that, precious kitten?"

In answer, Lina let out a feral moan that shot straight to his cock. Eagerly, she tugged him back to her mouth by his hair. They kissed, hot and wet—and it was *everything*. He walked her backwards to his bed, all the while devouring. His fingers trailed up the back of her dress, the cool teeth of its zipper tickling him. He stopped at the foot of the bed and pulled the zipper down, tracing the much hotter skin of her back on his way. She helped the effort with a shrug of her shoulders, sending the silky black fabric to pool at her feet.

Tony broke their kiss and stepped back to look his fill, delighting in the gooseflesh that erupted over her skin in the wake of his slow perusal. Her gorgeous, full breasts were contained in a scandalously sheer black lace brassiere; her shapely legs encased in black stockings that clipped to a pair of matching tap pants, which hugged her generously curved hips.

It was his turn to growl like an animal.

Lina reached out to grab the hem of his sweater, but he swatted her hands away and gently pushed her to sit on the bed, shaking his head in admonition. "This is about your reward, remember?"

The flash of excitement in her eyes warred with her pout. He pulled his sweater and undershirt off in one swift motion and grinned down at her. "Better?"

"Who's the show-off now?" she shot back, even as her fiery gaze scorched him.

He set his hands on his hips with an exaggerated flex. "Would you like me to put it back on?"

Molten gold eyes narrowed at him. "Don't you fucking dare."

With a chuckle, he knelt in front of her, unable to resist giving her a deep kiss along the way. Her fingers in his hair tempted him away from his task, but he refused to be derailed. Focused and unwavering, he unhooked the clasp of her bra and slid it off, tossing it behind him. He lifted both breasts in his hands, kneading one gently while bending his head to the other. Wasting no time, he sealed his lips over the entire tip while flicking his tongue over her tight nipple. Her resulting gasp was utter perfection to his ears.

"You like that, don't you?" he asked against her skin.

With her nod, her chest flexed under his mouth, and he continued his ministrations for another few heartbeats before letting go with an audible pop. Then waited until her eyes met his before speaking again.

"I wonder, though…" He dotted a few small kisses over her abdomen. "Is that enough of a reward for you, kitten?" Tony traced his finger along the same path his mouth had forged. "Or can I do better?"

Her plaintive mewl had him grinning wickedly.

"Oh, yeah. I can definitely do better."

Tony sat back on his haunches and removed her wedge heels one at a time. Taking his time, he trailed both hands over one calf and up to her thigh, and once he'd unclipped her stocking, he slid it down even more slowly, caressing the entire way. Lina was panting already, but he wasn't nearly finished.

When he turned to her other leg, he made quick work of unfastening the nylon, but then took the top of it between his teeth and pulled it gently over her skin.

Lina fell back onto her elbows. "Jaysus Christ, Tony."

His laugh nearly dislodged the sheer fabric from his mouth, but he held it together long enough to reach her ankle and pull it the rest of the way with his hands.

"Sorry." He was not, in fact, sorry at all. "Am I teasing you too much?"

Her eyes flashed in playful censure, but before she could answer, he took hold of her waistband and tugged her last remaining undergarment off over her hips. A quick glance at her face was the only warning he gave her before burying himself in the heaven between her legs.

Lina's cry could have woken the dead, and it spurred him on. He'd planned to take his time, but her swift sensitivity was irresistible. He flicked his tongue over her clit in a frantic rhythm, and he thought for sure she'd yank handfuls of his hair out by the roots. He'd never been harder in his life.

She was close, but not quite there, which was unacceptable to him. He thrust two fingers inside her, thrilled by the immediate clenching of her muscles around him. At the same time, he sealed his lips around her bud and sucked as if his life depended on it.

"Oh, shit. Tony!" Her exclamation descended into a low, keening, decidedly leopard-like roar.

As her orgasm crested on and on, he refused to let up, despite how close he was to spending in his pants. When she finally collapsed against the bed with a whimper, he withdrew his fingers and placed a kiss on her hip.

His own chest heaving, he rested his chin on her thigh with a grin. "*That's* a reward."

Lina's laughter shook her entire body and nearly dislodged him. "Come here, you."

She pulled at his shoulders, and he rose over her, pausing only to shed his trousers. He pushed her back against the bed as they lost themselves in a deep, drugging kiss. Given the force of her climax, he expected her to be more languid, but she raked her nails down his back and took a fierce hold of his ass, pressing him to her. His cock twitched almost painfully against her stomach.

"Do you have something?" Lina rasped.

"Mm-hmm." He closed his lips over the pulse at the base of her throat. "Ready for another reward so soon?"

"I was born ready." She pulled back to look at him, fireworks exploding in her eyes. "Do I need to do another trick to earn it?"

A growl roared from his chest, and he took her mouth ferociously. "You've more than earned it, sweetheart. Don't move."

It pained him to let go of her, but needs must. He dashed into his adjoining bathroom and grabbed a mercifully full tin of rubbers. He returned to find that Lina had, in fact, moved a bit. Not only was she now positioned more fully on his bed, but she'd flipped over onto all fours, and was arching her back in a luxurious stretch.

When she spotted him, her lips curved up and she held his gaze seductively while she slowly folded her arms and leaned down to rest her head on them. A move which pushed her lush ass higher…

"*Fuck*," he groaned. She chuckled, but they'd be lucky if he could get the condom on in time. Miraculously, he managed it. Tony climbed onto the bed behind her and sank into her with what he hoped was an approximation of grace. Judging by her moan, which echoed his, he'd done all right.

Once inside her, his desire to draw things out warred with his body's need for immediate detonation. The heat of her felt so damn perfect he wanted to stay there forever. He willed himself to thrust more slowly, savor as much as he could. The way she writhed against him didn't make it easy.

He tried to hold her hips steady beneath him, while he bent to gently bite at her shoulder.

"Goddesses, Tony," she whimpered.

He snaked one hand around to toy with her clit, but he'd only gotten in a few strokes when she clawed at his wrist, pushing him away as she straightened up. The motion dislodged him, and his cock wanted to protest. At the same time, concern flooded his chest.

Before he could utter a word, she twisted to face him and pushed him back on his heels. In one fluid move, she straddled his lap and sank back down to his hilt, making them both gasp.

The look in her eyes felled him completely.

Her need was clear—for pleasure, for release, yes. But also to see into the depths of him. And god, did he want to show all of it to her.

The upheaval of the last few days—his anxiety, his regret, his sheer shock, *everything*—evaporated, his focus narrowing to one pinpoint of light. *Lina.*

She snaked her arms around his neck, pulling his body closer, and he splayed one hand on her lower back and cradled the back of her head with his other. Their eyes remained locked; all the while their hips beat out an increasingly erratic rhythm. Wild noises escaped them both.

Tony watched in complete awe as not just her eyes, but her skin as well, took on what looked like—no, what he now knew *was*—a supernatural glow. She lit up from within, and he'd never wanted anything more than to burn up in her corona.

He shuddered his release, and she cried out hers, clenching tightly around him, only a moment later.

As they collapsed against each other, Tony knew with absolute certainty that his heart, his very soul, belonged to this glorious woman in his arms. And he never wanted to let go.

Chapter Thirteen

*L*ina's limbs felt utterly boneless as she lay on Tony's bed, catching her breath. He'd ducked into the bathroom to rid himself of the rubber, and she took advantage of his absence to calm her racing thoughts as well.

She'd *never* experienced an orgasm like that. She didn't know if it was due to her feelings for Tony himself, or the fact that he was the first person with whom she'd actually shared her secret, or some combination of both. But the force of her pleasure had almost been too much to bear.

And she'd never felt more connected to her magic.

The only thing holding her feet to the earth was the fact that Tony seemed to be experiencing a similar tidal wave. If she was going under, she found great comfort in the fact that at least she wasn't going alone.

When he returned, she summoned enough energy to take his place for a refresher of her own. Though her legs had a close call, nearly turning to jelly when he grabbed her hand in passing and brushed a sweet kiss over the back of it.

She emerged from the bathroom to find that he'd, unfortunately, put his undershorts back on, and was standing over their charming little dinner table with a furrowed brow.

She didn't care to put much of anything on, but she plucked Tony's sweater off the floor anyway and slipped it over her head. He wasn't particularly tall, but it still reached a good way down her thighs. And was rather cozy at that. Best of all, it smelled like him—warm and cedar-y.

Lina drew up next to him. "Everything okay?"

"No."

Oh.

He raised stricken eyes to her, and her heart sank. After his initial shock, he'd been so open and accepting of her revelations. Her body still hummed from everything they'd just done. *Too good to be true?*

"I'm sorry, Lina. One of these days, I *am* going to serve you a proper, hot meal. I promise."

Her laugh rode out on a wave of relief. "I don't know. It's kinda nice, actually." She gestured at their abandoned plates. "We're making a little tradition out of cold noodles."

His snort turned into a groan, and he hung his head.

"You're being far too hard on yourself," she added. "After all, it might not have been what you planned, but you did make a proper meal out of me." She slid her arms around the warm skin of his waist. "And that was plenty hot."

He returned her embrace. "I can't argue with you there."

Tony bent his head to kiss her, at the same moment her stomach decided to contradict her reassurances with an audible rumble. His echoing laugh warmed her despite her embarrassment.

"Okay, that's it. I'm feeding you for real, right now." He let her go to pick up their plates.

"Wait, what are you doing? I don't mind eating it cold."

He leveled her with a stern look. "Lina. I am not giving you cold food. Again. The steak might be beyond saving, but I can at least do something about the spaghetti. It'll only take a few minutes." She opened her mouth to protest, but he cut her off. "No arguments."

"Fine." She folded her arms across her chest in mock affront, before arching an eyebrow. "Do I at least get a reward if I don't argue?"

His brown eyes darkened with desire. "Maybe." With a smirk, he turned to the stairs, and she followed him down to the kitchen.

Tony paused in front of his stove, biting his lip enticingly. Before Lina could ask, he nodded, then slid their plates into the oven and turned it on. He peered into a sauce pot on top of the range, and lit the burner underneath it. With a shrug, he explained, "In case the oven dries everything out."

She grinned at his thoroughness. On her way to join him, her attention caught on a large, fur-filled basket on the floor. "Aww…" All seven kittens huddled in a giant pile, fast asleep.

Tony leaned one hip on the counter behind him. "They are pretty adorable when they take a break from being agents of chaos."

"Indeed." Lina left the cats to their repose and braced herself against the large worktable, facing Tony.

They watched each other, his small smile matching hers. She felt unaccountably shy all of a sudden.

"Lina, I…" The tips of his ears grew pink. "Can I ask you something?" He shook his head. "Sorry, I feel like I've done nothing but pepper you with questions."

"You've managed a few other activities…"

Her observation had the intended effect, and his shoulders relaxed. He raked a hot glance over her entire body, and his voice deepened deliciously. "And god, Lina. Those activities were … extraordinary."

Lina shivered. "They were."

He cleared his throat. "That's what I wanted to ask about, actually. When we were nearing the finish line, was it just me, or did I see…" He paused, considering his words. "I thought I noticed … something like what happened earlier, with Betty. Like … I could see your magic?"

Instinctively, she held her breath and braced for the dropping of the other shoe. Which was silly. Because Tony watched her with nothing but fascination and desire. She shoved aside her doubts and found her voice. "I admit I was a bit distracted at the time..." His answering grin, tinged with pride, warmed her even further. "But I did think something might be happening."

"Does it always?"

"It doesn't. As a matter of fact ... it's never happened before."

"Oh. Wow." He appeared positively thunderstruck. In the best way.

It inspired her to keep talking. "I've always tended to keep my affairs more physical than emotional." She fiddled with the cuff of his sweater, its softness comforting against her skin. "Easier, I suppose, when there's a big part of yourself you have to keep a lid on."

His sympathetic hum was laced with an undercurrent of chivalrous outrage on her behalf.

"What you said yesterday, about us unlocking some kind of sex magic?"

Tony groaned. "Please don't remind yourself. God, I was such an ass."

She reached over to trace a consoling fingertip down his chest. "We've established that I threw a lot at you. And you offered one hell of an apology."

He caught her hand and kissed it, then turned to give the sauce a quick stir.

"But," she continued, "you might not have been entirely wrong, at that."

He faced her fully, eyebrows raised in silent question.

"I wasn't lying when I said I've had these powers since long before I met you. And truly, nothing like this has ever happened to me before. But..." She rubbed her thumbnail over her bottom lip. "My magic seems to ... respond to you. A lot."

"Does that happen to everyone in your ... clan? Family? Group?"

She smiled. "Most often, we refer to ourselves as a coven. And no. Not that I know of."

"Huh. Really?"

Lina shrugged. "You know I didn't exactly apply myself to my studies. But trust me, if I'd gotten any hint of sex magic being involved? *That* would've inspired me to pay attention."

Tony laughed heartily at that, and she joined him before sobering again. "It's more than just the sex, to be honest. What happened upstairs might be the most extreme example, but my magic has been going a bit haywire ever since we met. Granted, that was the same day Alice turned the reins over to me, so I suppose it could have something to do with pulling my powers out of retirement, but…"

He reached over and took her hand, his thumb rubbing soothingly. "But?"

"It feels like my magic … heightens with you. Specifically you." She turned her hand over in his, giving him a little squeeze. "Earlier, when I was projecting comfort into Betty, and you held my hand? It's hard to describe, but I felt something extra. Like my connection to you was enhancing my magic somehow."

Tony sucked in a sharp inhale. "Wow. I'm…" He smiled shyly. "I'm honored, Lina. To have earned not only your trust, but … your magic's too."

Lina swallowed around the lump in her throat. "You're too much, you know that?" Before he could answer, she pulled him in for a kiss, happy to linger in the taste, the feel of him.

In what was becoming a pattern between them, it didn't take long for the tide to turn in passion's favor. For their kiss to grow messier, more heated. Tony surprised her by wrenching himself away.

"Uh-uh. I'm not letting you distract me again." He raked a hand through his already mussed hair. "I promised you a hot meal, not a burnt one."

Her laugh bubbled up. "Fair enough."

She relished the way the thin fabric of his shorts pulled across his ass as he bent to retrieve their food from the oven. He'd just begun ladling extra sauce over both dishes when Lina felt a soft nudge at her ankle. Her grin widened. A sleepy Gouda blinked up at her, purring softly as she rubbed against Lina's leg.

"Well, look who's awake." She bent to scoop up the kitten. "I hate to disappoint you, but the spaghetti's not for you."

Tony glanced over his shoulder. "It most certainly is not. Her treats are over there, though."

Lina gave a *tsk*, even as she followed his direction. "And you wonder why she keeps trying to get away with murder." She couldn't resist punctuating her statement with a pinch of his outstanding ass.

"Hey!" He flicked a dishtowel against her leg, descending them both into laughter. Even Gouda joined in with a tiny meow, which only made them cackle harder.

Lina not only gave her an extra treat, she carried her upstairs with them and let her snuggle on her lap while she and Tony ate their dinner. Which turned out to be delicious, despite its delay. Even the filet mignon wasn't ruined.

By the time they finished, night had fully fallen and the candlelight, while romantic, was growing a bit too dim. Tony got up to flick on a lamp, then paused by the window on his way back. Lina watched the firm muscles of his still-shirtless back bunch on a sigh. She followed him over, dropping a dozing Gouda on the window seat before wrapping her arms around him from behind.

"Betty will be all right," Lina whispered against his shoulder.

He settled his hands over hers. "I hope so. I just feel so help-less, you know?" He heaved another sigh. "But what you did earlier, that did seem to make her feel better."

"It felt like it did. And I'll keep trying."

"Thanks," he murmured.

Lina hummed as a thought occurred to her. "I wonder…"

"What?"

"I'm just thinking about what you, *we*, seem to inspire in my magic. Given the nature of Betty's ailment, her missing Bob and all… Maybe there's something in that. Something more I can do." She leaned her chin against his back. "I only wish I knew what it was. Or that I could talk it over with Alice." Beneath Tony's hand, she absently rubbed at her ring. "But as important as this is…"

"It's not enough of a crisis to pull her away from what she's doing." He lifted her hand and kissed her knuckle, right below her ring. "I get it. I appreciate what you are doing, Lina." He let go and turned to face her, his expression skeptical. "So you really think her problem is … Bob-related?"

"Of course. What, you're allowed to go steady, but she's not?"

Tony opened his mouth to protest, but Lina cut him off with a chuckle. She tugged him down to sit on the window seat and threaded her arm through his.

"I know," she continued, "leopards don't typically form bonds like that. And sure, in the wild, with lots of choices, who can blame them?" That got a smile out of him. "But Betty's lived among humans her entire life. Bob is the first of her kind she's ever gotten to spend time with, right?"

"He is."

"I'm guessing he's got a similar story. It'd be strange if they *didn't* get attached to each other."

Tony huffed. "And given the noises we heard the last time we sat here…" He paused, his gaze going intense for a moment as they both remembered that lovely occasion. He shook his head. "I should've seen it coming. I just…"

"Didn't expect it to hit her this hard?"

"No," he said quietly, before groaning in defeat. "God, I never should have let those goons take Bob."

"Tony. You weren't here when it happened."

"I should've been."

"You can't put yourself under house arrest. And even if you'd been around, what would you have done? Argued with them? Not let Bob out of his pen? That would've angered them, and based on all you've told me, put you all at risk."

He wrapped his arm around her shoulders and pulled her close. "You're right. I know you are."

Lina hugged him back. "I usually am."

Tony's chest rumbled with a chuckle. "I'm learning that." He kissed the crown of her head. After a beat, he said, "Circus jackasses aside… You think, essentially, our best course of action to help Betty is to reunite her with Bob?"

"I'd say so. You and Carl haven't found any dirt on the circus yet, have you?"

"No. I've been tempted to call the cops with an anonymous tip, just make something up, but who knows if it'd work. They're liable to figure out it's me, and then I'd be in deeper shit."

"Plus, there's no guarantee Bob would end up back here with you, at least not right away."

He grunted in agreement.

"What if we stage a jailbreak?" she asked. "Bust Bob out of the pokey?"

Tony snorted. "If only."

"Why not?"

He pulled back to stare at her. "Because we're likely to end up in 'the pokey' ourselves?"

"They wouldn't have to know it was us." She smirked up at him. "I do have some skills at my disposal."

"Lina." He took her by the shoulders. "You cannot do that." He held up a hand, forestalling her argument. "I am not doubting your abilities. But what if something goes wrong? What happens if you get caught, in either form? By the circus, or … hell, Animal Control? Then what?" He raised one eyebrow. "If the press finds out…?"

She scrunched her nose in defeat. "Okay, you've got me there."

"Seriously, though. Promise me you won't take this on yourself. I … I couldn't stand it if anything happened to you."

The raw concern in his eyes melted her completely. "I promise."

He held her gaze for another moment before nodding. "We

just need to keep digging. Guys like that must have skeletons in the closet."

"I can ask Alice when she gets back, too. I know they were on her radar to begin with, so maybe she can help."

"Thanks." He exhaled. "And hopefully your comforting magic can get Betty through the screen test in the meantime."

She kissed his cheek. "I'll do my best."

He pulled her close again, and she nestled into him with a contented purr. The more time she spent with Tony, the less it bothered her that her inner cat made such an audible appearance around him.

His amused huff ruffled the hair at her temple. "Have I mentioned how much I love it when you purr?"

She gave in and rumbled again, more purposely this time, and delighted in his laughter.

Tony suddenly stiffened. "Your sounds. Lina, maybe that's it."

Lina straightened and shot him a questioning look.

"Don't you see? Betty's calls, the last time we were here. What if that could snap her out of it now? If she hears Bob?"

"Bob's not here."

"No. But you are."

Despite his hopeful look, Lina still struggled to catch up. "You've lost me."

He sat up more fully, gesturing animatedly. "It's like that movie, the one Nick was worried about. You know, with Grant and Hepburn? Wasn't there some screwy business with people trying to make leopard calls, and the leopard calling back?"

"I think so…"

"So what if you mimic Bob? It might improve her spirits, right?"

Lina bit her lip, as she finally understood him. She hated to burst his bubble, but…

"Tony, I don't think that'll work. For starters, I can't 'speak leopard' as myself, and even if I could, every leopard's call is distinctive. Betty's a smart cat. As much as I appreciate your faith in my acting skill, she'll recognize it's not him."

"That's true." His shoulders slumped as he glanced out the window. Betty's silhouette was just visible in the moonlight. "And if we did manage to fool her, what would it do to her if Bob didn't show up then?"

Lina cupped his cheek, a shadow of stubble rasping her palm. "It was a good idea in theory."

"Just not in practice." He let out a rueful laugh.

"I'm sorry." She brushed his hair off his forehead. "Listen. If worse comes to worst, I'll make some excuse. Call in sick or something, and do the screen test myself. We'll get you two that job."

Tony feathered a kiss over her lips. "Thank you, Lina."

She wrapped her arms around him and held him tight, determined, despite her trepidation, to make good on her promise. For all of them.

Chapter Fourteen

heir continued brainstorming over the next few days yielded no concrete, or legal, ideas to spring Bob from his circus lockup before the screen test. Lina's efforts helped Betty show signs of improvement, but the leopard was hardly back to performance level, and it broke Lina's heart that she hadn't been more successful.

When it came time for the big day, Lina arrived at the ranch, ready to make her excuses and sneak off to replace Betty if absolutely necessary—because it just might be.

She immediately spotted Tony's truck, but saw no sign of him or his leopard. It was a big enough ranch, and she hadn't heard where exactly they'd be set up for the test. She grabbed her bag with every intention of finding him before checking in with the production folks, but no sooner had she reached the edge of the parking area than Opal Prince, the head of Makeup at Phoenix—and, Lina recalled, a friend of Tony's—found her.

Opal called out with a cheerful wave. "Lina, hi! Almost perfect timing—I was just heading back to my trailer to clean up and get things laid out for your project. You're with me today."

"Wow, they brought out the big guns for a simple screen test? I thought Betty was the real star today, not me."

The makeup artist shrugged. "I've been supervising *Tumble-weeds at Midnight*, and doing Yvette's makeup, so I agreed to stick around and get you ready." She leaned in conspiratorially. "And to cheer Tony on. It'd be so great if he got this."

"It would." Lina fought her nerves as she followed Opal in the direction of the small village of trailers on the outskirts of the complex.

"He and I have been friends for a while, and I can tell you, he's one of the good ones." Opal paused. "Forgive me if I'm butting in, since it's technically none of my business, but I get the impression you two have been spending a lot of time together?"

Lina swallowed, unsure where this was going. "We have."

"I'm glad. Tony deserves some happiness in his life. And some fun." Opal's grin was infectious. "I know you and I haven't had the chance to spend much time together yet, on or off set—which we must fix—but you seem like a quality dame yourself."

Lina laughed. "Thanks."

"You are quite welcome. Anyway, I'm rooting for you two crazy kids."

"I appreciate that," Lina replied, her cheeks heating from more than the sunshine. She glanced at their surroundings. "Speaking of... Have you seen him yet?"

"No, he's probably still setting up. They've got you guys over in that corner, so they don't need to move the equipment too far." She smiled reassuringly. "Why don't you get yourself settled, and then go find him while I lay out my supplies?"

"Sounds great."

Opal pointed her in the direction of her assigned trailer. Lina found a pair of sample costumes waiting for her, but since she didn't know which they wanted her in to start—and in case she needed to make a quick, non-wardrobe-related transformation first—she changed into a robe. Leaving on her closed-toed flats in anticipation of the ranch's dirt and gravel, she set out to search for Tony.

It didn't take her long. Production had converted a horse pen into a staging area for Betty, next to a few building facades near the edge of the property. She caught a quick glimpse of Betty's spotted coat among the bustle of crew members back and forth in front of the pen. Tony was much harder to miss, with the sunlight burnishing his hair a more fiery auburn than usual. He turned in her direction—and her heart skipped at the sight of his broad, bright smile.

"Lina!" He rushed over to her.

"Hi. How are things?"

"You wouldn't believe…" He reached out to touch her, but stopped himself with a quick glance around them. "Damn. You think it'll mess with our chances if I take you in my arms right now?" he whispered.

Longing flooded her, and she almost gave in. "We probably shouldn't risk it. Though I take it, from your enthusiasm, that Betty's in good shape today?"

Tony's grin took on an edge of disbelief. "I almost hate to say it out loud, but … Lina, she's back to her old self. She did a couple of practice tricks before we'd even left Applegate. And she's taking all this in like a champ. If it was possible, I'd almost swear I saw her *smile*."

A surprised laugh bubbled up out of Lina. "Tony, that's fantastic! What snapped her out of it, I wonder?"

He spread his arms in a wide shrug. "I have no idea. I'm willing to bet, though, that a lot of it's down to you."

"When I left yesterday, she was hardly better."

"But you've been…" He lowered his voice. "…doing your thing an awful lot. Maybe it's cumulative." One side of his mouth kicked up. "Whatever it is, I'm not about to look a gift leopard in the mouth."

They both snickered as he led her over to Betty's makeshift enclosure. Sure enough, the leopard sat up, tail twitching playfully, while she watched the flurry of activity around her with a calm, bright expression. When they reached the fence, Betty rose and loped directly over to Lina.

"Hi, Betty." Lina reached through the fence to scratch her behind the ears. "Look at you, all camera-ready." Betty rumbled contentedly. "I am so happy to see you like this, lady."

The cat nudged affectionately at Lina's hand, then turned and padded off to the other side of the pen, tail raised jauntily in the air.

Lina blinked in surprise. "Wow."

"I know." Tony's eyes danced with barely contained glee, and as he glanced down her body, his smile took on a different kind of warmth. "Nice robe."

She'd chosen her favorite—leopard-print satin—especially for the occasion. "Thought it might bring us some luck. Dressing the part, and all that."

Tony's lips parted, but whatever quip he'd been about to make was drowned out by a noise from the pen beside them. A very loud, very distinct—and rather *horny*—sound.

Their heads whipped around to Betty, sitting rather primly on her haunches given the circumstances. If she hadn't witnessed the leopard's mouth closing over the last notes of her cry, Lina might have doubted it even happened. When she glanced back at Tony, his face was frozen in a shocked mask that doubtless mirrored her own.

"Did she just...?" Lina breathed.

"Uh-huh."

"I'm no expert, but that sounded an awful lot like a..."

"It did." Tony rubbed a hand over his jaw. "It would explain a lot. But ... how...?"

"That sounded enthusiastic!" A booming voice startled them.

Lina and Tony turned to find Peabody approaching. She'd worked with the man once before and knew him to be talented, but highly understated, in his reactions. His current cheer was encouraging, if a bit unnerving.

"Miss Leonard, Mr. Benson. Good to see you both." He nodded at them in turn, then focused on Betty. "Someone sounds ready. I say, that was a happy sound, wasn't it?"

Tony's voice cracked as he answered. "Yes. Of course. Very happy."

Peabody rubbed his hands together. "Excellent."

Before any of them could say more, a second cry sounded, slightly deeper and more rumbling … and emanating from the direction of the trees. Behind them.

Tony met Lina's stunned stare with a vaguely panicked expression. Peabody didn't notice their behavior—but that was because his gaze was locked on Betty, his brow furrowed in confusion. He opened his mouth, ostensibly to ask why the hell hers hadn't moved.

Lina blurted, "My word! I had no idea this part of the canyon had such a fantastic echo."

Peabody's lips formed a near-perfect *o* as he glanced first at her, then their surroundings. "Neither did I."

With the director's attention now focused elsewhere, Tony shot Lina a silent *what the hell?* expression. She shrugged. Who cared how preposterous the excuse sounded, as long as it did the trick?

Peabody shook off his befuddlement with a hum. "You know, that might be useful. I hadn't planned to use sound today, but perhaps we should. Can she do that on cue?"

Tony made a choked sound. "Um, I'm not sure. We can try."

"Great. Excuse me." Peabody strode off to confer with the crew.

After a stunned beat, Tony spoke in a hushed rasp. "Please tell me you perfected ventriloquism skills overnight."

"You have no idea how much I wish I had."

In unison, they pivoted to face the tree line where the bonus call had come from.

"An echo? Really?"

"He bought it, didn't he?" she hissed.

Tony grunted his agreement.

"Sooo…" Lina began, "do we think that was Bob?"

"Most likely."

"*How*? I kept my word, I swear. I didn't go anywhere near that circus."

"I know." Tony nodded, his trust in her gratifying, as he continued scanning the trees. "God, I haven't the foggiest. I doubt they just … let him go."

"No. He must've escaped?" A simultaneously terrible and inspiring thought struck her. "Hey, Gouda was with us the other night when we talked about Bob. You don't think she…?"

"What? Made it all the way down to the Valley, navigated a circus, picked a lock, and then got back to the sanctuary in one piece?" He raised an eyebrow at her.

Lina shrugged defensively. "She is a crafty little lass. If anyone could, it'd be her."

Tony's snort descended into a groan. "What are we gonna do? The minute another leopard bursts through those trees, all hell will break loose around here."

"Keep our fingers crossed that he resists the urge to burst?"

They exchanged a glance, then sighed together. Peabody's voice pulled them away from any further strategizing.

"Great news, we can wire Betty for sound." The director paused. "Well, not actually wire her, but you get the idea."

"Great," Tony echoed, his voice less than steady.

Peabody continued on blithely. "We should be ready to go in a few minutes. As discussed, we'll start with a few preliminary shots of Betty by herself. Mr. Benson, let's keep you just outside of frame while you lead her through…"

His words faded into the background, just as Lina noticed a shadowy movement out of the corner of her eye. A *spotted* shadowy movement, lingering inside the edge of the trees. Slowly, so as not to attract attention, she turned toward the wooded area, and…

Fuuuuuck.

She grabbed Tony's arm, her nails digging into his bicep. When Peabody mercifully called out to a passing lighting grip,

Tony sent her a puzzled look. She jerked her head behind and mouthed, "*Bob.*"

His eyes went saucer-wide as they focused over her shoulder. "Shit."

A plan—and perhaps her life—flashed before her.

"Listen," she whispered, "you keep everyone, including Betty, distracted. I'll take care of Bob."

His gaze whipped back to her. "What?"

She kept one eye on Peabody while she rushed on. "I'll lead him back into the woods, tie him to a tree or something, and keep him hidden until the screen test is over."

Tony's mouth gaped open as his eyes slid back and forth between the distracted director in front of them and the potentially randy leopard behind her. "How the hell are you going to manage that?"

"Did you forget who you're talking to?" She held up the collar of her robe, in all its leopard-print glory.

He shook his head with concern-laden skepticism.

She infused her voice with confidence. "Trust me."

"I do." With a huff, he nodded in Bob's direction. "It's *him* I'm not so sure about."

"That's settled." Peabody's voice pierced their fraught little bubble. The two of them whipped around in surprise, but luckily the man had yet to notice the feline-shaped elephant in the room. "So if you could start getting Betty ready…" he continued.

"Well, that's my cue," Lina interjected. She gave Tony's arm a reassuring squeeze, then clapped her hands together and pasted on a bright smile. "I'll leave you to it, dash over to Makeup and see if Opal's ready for me. See you!"

Tony bit his lip with a worried look, but nodded, and peppered Peabody with questions as he animatedly led him over to Betty.

Only then did Lina exhale. She could handle this.

She hoped.

Backing away, she stooped to swipe a rope from the ground

next to Betty's pen when no one was looking, and marched toward the cat hovering at the tree line.

"FOR FUCK'S SAKE, Bob, throw me a bone, would ya?"

Lina huffed upward in an attempt to dislodge the lock of hair that had fallen in her face for the umpteenth time, at the same time tugging futilely at the rope with both hands. She'd been at this for nearly fifteen minutes; to say that Bob had budged even a few feet would be putting it generously.

He was one damn immovable leopard.

She might be a little impatient, but patience was a luxury she couldn't afford at the moment.

A blast of calming magic had allowed Lina to slip the rope around Bob rather quickly, but her success proved too good to last. Every time she got him to take a few steps, he promptly stopped and turned in Betty's direction yet again. She suspected that whoever coined the "one step forward" adage had spent time with Bob.

She was sorely tempted to see if he'd follow her in her leopard form instead, but the way her day was going, she was liable to attract the wrong kind of attention from him. The last thing she needed was Betty turning on her for stealing her boyfriend.

Instead, Lina inhaled deeply, summoned more of her power, and pushed the spark along the rope and into Bob. Then nearly fell on her ass when her next tug yielded zero results.

She bent at the waist and braced her hands on her knees, groaning.

"Shit like this is why I went into acting," she grumbled aloud.

Her efforts with Betty had lured her into a false sense of accomplishment. Except … she hadn't been too successful there either, had she? True, she'd comforted Betty, but it was Bob's appearance that finally returned Betty to herself.

Lina shook her head. She simply lacked practice—and really

should've paid more bloody attention to her studies back in the day. Her magic had been plenty strong with Tony around; too bad she couldn't enlist his help now. But he had his hands full. For all their sakes, she needed to do this herself.

Although… The very thought of Tony sent a new zing down her spine. *Okay, use this.* She shook out her shoulders and straightened, taking a firmer hold on the rope. Closing her eyes briefly, she called to mind an image of Tony guiding Betty through her tricks. It instantly made her smile, and a corresponding rush of magic sparked along her skin.

She opened her eyes to find Bob's attention on her. *Finally.*

"Come on, buddy," she crooned softly. "You want to help your gal, don't you?"

The leopard flicked his head in the wrong direction, but then— miracle of miracles—he lifted a paw and took a tentative step toward Lina.

"Okay. *Okay.*" She held Tony and Betty firm in her thoughts, pulsing her affection for both of them outward. Even though Bob couldn't understand her words, she continued speaking. "Betty needs this job, pal. And you want what's best for her, right?" Another step. "You're not one of those gents who stifles your love's ambitions. You're worthy of our lass, aren't you?"

Lina kept up a running commentary until they'd traveled far enough from the ranch's clearing for comfort. *Thank the goddesses.* She came to a tentative stop, ready to breathe a sigh of relief, and Bob watched her for a moment—then smoothly swung back around to face the ground they'd just covered.

"Fuck me," she muttered.

She planted herself in front of him, blocking his path. Without letting go of the rope, she fisted her hands on her hips. His nostrils flared slightly, which was probably not the best sign, all things considered. But she stood her ground.

"Bob, love. Listen to me. I know you want to be with Betty. I get it, believe me. I'd love nothing more than to pull Tony behind one of those facades and have my way with him. But we can't do that right now." She paused, looking skyward with a sigh. "I'm talking sex with a leopard. *What* is my life coming to?"

Bob assessed her with an expression that said much the same, and she fought the urge to hiss at him.

"Look, pal. Those two need us. And I promise, if you just stay here for a little bit, I'll let you go back to her and get as frisky as you want. Deal?"

Because he was a bloody leopard, and not a human being with a remote grasp of the English language, Bob responded by focusing his attention behind her. Looking suspiciously as if he planned to make a run for it.

"Goddess, this is so fucking exhausting." Lina pinched the bridge of her nose.

Exhausting. A memory, distant and blurry, called to her. Of lessons, half-learned. A footnote in her adolescence, its print tiny, but if she squinted her mind's eye…

There's magic for that.

Perhaps she'd paid more attention than she realized. Determination burned through her fatigue, and she tapped into her feelings for Tony—and Bob's for Betty—once more.

The first wave of her magic crested, and Bob's focus returned to her for a fraction of a second, before going hazy altogether. He blinked drowsily up at her, and she reined in a whoop of satisfaction.

"That's right, good boy." She couldn't help adding, "You're getting verrrry sleepy…"

As Bob's eyelids fluttered, she snorted. All she was missing was a pocket watch to swing in front of him.

Only another couple of pulses, and Bob lowered himself to the ground, his head lolling forward to rest on his front paws. She'd never heard a more perfect sound than the subsequent rumbling of his snores.

"There. That should hold you for…" She had no clue how long, actually, but no time to worry about it.

She'd guided Bob to his nap near enough to a modest-sized

tree, so now she looped the end of the rope around it in her best approximation of a tight knot. She glanced around as she finished. Better not to take any chances.

The sparks inside her were fading fast, but she summoned enough for a mediocre finale, hiding the slumbering leopard with a glamouring cast. Her shoulders sagged in relief, and with her hands finally free, she raked her brunette waves back off her face once and for all.

Or so she thought. By the time she finally arrived at the makeup trailer, after having gotten lost several times—the woods were far more complex than they looked—Lina's fingers had made rather a messy tangle of her hair. And she preferred not to think about the colossal layer of dust now coating her shoes and the hem of her robe.

Opal greeted her from the doorway of the Makeup trailer. "I was about to send out a search party." Her eyebrows crept upward as she took in Lina's disheveled, weary state. "Damn, what happened to you?"

Lina's cheeks heated. "Oh, um… I got a bit lost on my way back here." She used her acting skills to flash a reassuring smile.

Opal snickered. "Wonder what Tony looks like…" She gestured her inside with a wink. "Come on, I'll fix ya right up."

Lina had more excuses ready, but if Opal thought she'd been off somewhere making whoopee with Tony… Well, that was a hell of a lot better explanation than the truth, so she let it stand.

As she surrendered to Opal's capable hands, Lina finally released all the tension of the last few hours—hell, the last several days. The generous makeup artist fixed up not only her face, but her hair as well; she'd let the hairstylists go early, owing to their long filming schedule and the simplicity of Lina's needs for the screen test.

After a solid session of pampering and amiable small talk, Lina felt like a human being again.

Opal had just begun applying a final layer of powder when an ominous shiver ran through Lina's entire body—her magic, anything but warm or satisfying. Her citrine ring suddenly felt heavier on her finger. *A warning.*

"Lina? Is something wrong?" Opal paused, her makeup brush hovering over Lina's cheekbone.

"I'm not sure." Her chest felt tight, uncomfortable. "Excuse me a minute?"

She rose without waiting for a reply and stepped out of the trailer. Lina paused, waiting. Listening. Another shiver, bigger this time. Then male voices, raised in anger. One she didn't recognize, but the other…

Tony.

Shit.

Lina descended the last step of the trailer and took off into the trees, chasing her instincts. She couldn't decipher the words or the context, but Tony's voice was getting louder, closer. She dimly hoped Opal hadn't chosen to follow her, but she couldn't afford to stop and find out. Not with Tony—and dammit, she sensed Betty too—in danger.

She willed her legs, and hell, even her magic, to carry her faster. Almost there. She paused to get her bearings, ready to do … something. Anything. And then, all at once…

A deep, rumbling growl.

An ominous laugh.

A menacing voice. "I promise you, we'll be leaving with a leopard today."

Power surged, stronger than she'd ever experienced. Thoughts fell away. Hesitation vanished. Calm fury rose, at once cool and white-hot.

Lina flung off her robe and leapt.

Chapter Fifteen

"*L*ike hell you will." Tony's pulse sped up as Betty added her own reply, sharp teeth bared around the most menacing sound he'd ever heard from her. *Good girl.*

He should've known better than to lead her so far from the faux western town for her break. They'd only been out here a few minutes when Ralph, circus jerk extraordinaire, appeared—all cold, calculating eyes and a grimace twisting his lips. Along with his second-in-command, a dim, weaselly little fellow named Joey.

And neither one of them was buying Tony's evasion over Bob's whereabouts.

Ralph stood his ground, ignoring Betty's continued growling. "I'd say that's more than a fair exchange, wouldn't you?"

The words were barely out of the thug's mouth when salvation exploded out of the trees to their right. In the space of an instant, she sliced through the air in a smooth arc and came to a gracefully vicious landing directly in front of him and Betty. Her snarling roar practically shook the ground beneath them.

Tony's chest swelled with pride, and more love than he'd ever felt in his life, at the sight of this leopard warrior-queen before him.

Lina was utterly magnificent, in every form she took.

"A-ha!" Joey shouted. "We knew you took 'im!"

Joey definitely wasn't the brains of the operation, but he couldn't possibly think Lina was *Bob*, could he? *You almost believed she was Betty…* Tony swallowed.

"No idea where my leopard is, eh?" Ralph snarled.

Shit. "That's not—"

Without taking her eyes off Ralph, Lina cut Tony's protest off with another fierce growl. He hated to admit it, but she was right —he couldn't reveal her mistaken identity.

"Hey, maybe we oughta take *both* leopards!" Joey piped up.

Tony's growling drowned out hers. *No…*

"Whaddya know? You do get a good idea once in a while, Joey." Ralph's smile grew even more ominous as he extended a hand to Joey. "Gimme the tranq gun."

No.

Tony sucked in a breath, pulse spiking higher than ever. This was his worst nightmare, coming to life. He refused to let anything happen to Lina and Betty. But fuck it all, what if he couldn't stop it?

Miraculously, Frick and Frack began arguing over the dart gun. Joey had pulled it from the back of his waistband, but held it close to his chest.

"But boss, I only brought the one dart."

"What?" Ralph bellowed. "I told you to grab a bunch! You know you're a lousy shot!"

How these clowns could be so simultaneously bumbling and menacing, Tony had no clue. Though he much preferred bumbling, especially when Ralph sprang into action.

"Gimme that." He grabbed the gun. "Bob's our moneymaker. And a cranky bastard. We use this on him." Still mistaking her for Bob, he waved the weapon vaguely at Lina.

No no no no no…

Tony made a feral noise, taking marginal solace in the fact that it at least drew Ralph's attention back to him.

"Make this easy on yourself and get the hell out of the way, pal. We don't have to do this the hard way."

"We're not doing *this* at all," Tony hissed.

Ralph smirked, alarmingly calm. "How are you gonna stop me?"

Tony's mind raced. He had decent reflexes, so he might be able to shove one of them out of the way in time, but he didn't know who Ralph would aim for first. And while there were plenty of people nearby, calling out for help might make these two even more trigger happy.

Not to mention the fact that he had no idea what would happen to Lina's powers if, god forbid, she did get hurt. She might just transform right in front of everyone.

Terror shuddered through him.

Lina chose that moment to arch her back and take a bold step in front of Betty, tensed and ready to spring. *No!* Everything in him wanted to shout, to hold her back. His trust in her abilities warred with his desperation to see her safe, and said trust eked out a narrow victory. He believed she could take care of herself and, in turn, them.

But if he was able to somehow talk these goons down, maybe he could save her from having to act in the first place.

Tony inhaled sharply to do just that, but when he opened his mouth, the sound that followed wasn't his. Nor did it come from Lina. Or even Betty, despite its similarity to what she'd let out earlier.

No, this rumble came from the trees to their left. Tony wasn't sure whether to feel relief or even more panic. The situation was dire enough without adding a third leopard into the mix—and an unpredictable one at that.

Judging by their faces, Ralph and Joey heard the sound too. Lina took advantage of their distraction to send a glance over her shoulder at him, her eyes very much still *hers*. And filled with an alarming mix of worry and apology. But a sense of déjà vu hit Tony square in the chest, and he seized on the lifeline. *It might be worth a shot…* As if hearing his thought, Lina nodded her leopard head.

Joey'll fall for it, at least.

Tony mimicked Lina's earlier attempt with Peabody. "These woods have some echo."

Ralph let out a skeptical grunt. "That was no echo." He narrowed his eyes at Betty and Lina. "How did…?"

"I don't know, boss…" Joey squinted at the trees—*above* them for some unfathomable reason. He pointed up at the leaves. "I heard it on a radio show once. Cover like that pushes sound…"

Tony tuned out the man's droning and scrambled to come up with anything to get them all out of this. Keeping his head still, he darted his eyes over to where he'd heard Bob…

Fucking hell.

The leopard was indeed prowling toward them. *Or was he?*

Tony blinked a few times, staring at … nothing? He could have sworn Bob was right there. Betty whuffed in surprise, while Lina kept her attention trained on Ralph.

Who had just smacked Joey upside the head to curb his litany of useless information. *Good, they didn't notice anything.* Tony tugged a light warning on Betty's lead and adopted an innocent expression.

"Enough," Ralph hissed at him. He raised the tranq gun and aimed it squarely at Tony. "You've given me nothing but headaches. So you're gonna let us walk out of here with our leopard. And yours."

"Not a chance," Tony ground out. "I—"

"Hey, Ralphie, look!"

All their heads whipped in the direction Joey pointed—where Bob did *not* currently stand.

"Wait. It was just…" Joey's confusion was evident, and Tony didn't know whether to be relieved or highly troubled over the fact that he'd just had the same experience.

"I swear, Joey—" Ralph's voice trailed off in a choke.

Tony stared in morbid fascination as Bob appeared again …

sort of. He padded drowsily toward them, with a ghostly countenance. Fading eerily in and out, wavering as if…

As if someone magical glamoured him, and now it's wearing off.

He suppressed a sudden, absurd desire to laugh. Lina let out a frustrated grunt that, luckily, only he was close enough to hear. Clearly, this hadn't been part of her plan. Bob lumbered to a hazy stop a few feet away from them.

Joey's gaze darted back and forth between Bob and the two leopards in front of him, his mouth hanging comically open. At his side, Ralph stood, frozen, eyes narrowed as if he couldn't quite believe what he was seeing. Tony held his breath, debating the wisdom of making a lunge for the dart gun.

"The hell…?" Ralph muttered.

Fortunately—or unfortunately, depending on how one looked at it—the man's voice set off a reaction in Bob. He'd been blinking sleepily in their general direction, but something in Ralph caused the big cat to snap to attention, and he finally solidified. His focus zeroed in on Betty, and he dashed to her side, aiming a fierce growl at his former captors that rivaled Lina's.

Lina and Betty both joined in the snarling, and Lina's fur took on a subtle, shimmering cast. And then, in perfect unison, the trio took a single, beautiful, menacing step toward Joey and Ralph.

Joey promptly fell on his ass with a high-pitched yelp. Finally showing some fear, Ralph dropped the tranq gun and stumbled back, nearly tripping over Joey in the process. Only Lina continued to growl quietly, as Betty and Bob flanked her like loyal sentinels.

Tony's heart had never felt bigger.

Ralph's head swiveled among the menagerie, eyes wide and bravado gone. "Three leopards? *Three?* What the hell?"

"Fuck this, it ain't worth it anymore. I'm outta here!" Joey used Ralph for leverage to scramble to his feet, then immediately shoved him out of the way and charged away through the woods. Ralph, in turn, righted himself with a sound that was half-grunt, half-scream, and took off after his partner.

A bark of pure, delighted laughter burst out of Tony.

Lina's rumble was far less celebratory. She continued to stare after Ralph and Joey, posture tensed and ready to strike, apparently tempted to chase them down. Only Betty and Bob inching closer, one spotted head butting her affectionately on each side, finally relaxed her. She nuzzled them back with a huff before turning her head to look at him.

Her gorgeous eyes held triumph and concern in equal measure. Tony nodded at her, letting a grin spread over his face.

The air sparked and wavered, and the next thing he knew, Lina's body returned to its equally glorious human form. She remained in a crouch, petting both leopards' heads.

"Are you all right?" Her piercing, golden gaze lifted to him. "All of you?"

Tony nodded, his relief staggering. "We're fine. Thanks to you and Bob."

Lina's cheeks flushed prettily, though a hint of embarrassment crept into her expression. He stepped toward her, ready to swoop her into his arms, when someone delicately cleared her throat. Opal—*where the hell had she come from?*—hovered at the edge of the clearing, holding Lina's robe.

"Sorry to interrupt, but I got worried after a few minutes and followed you. I think you dropped this."

She tossed the garment to Lina, who caught it handily, then stood and swiftly donned it.

"Um, thanks, Opal." Lina eyed her cautiously.

Opal, for her part, simply nodded. It was highly unlikely she'd come upon them without seeing at least *something* of what had just transpired; yet she was cool as a cucumber. Tony frowned in confusion, and exchanged a worried glance with Lina.

But Betty's sudden huff pulled their attention. The leopard nudged Lina's hip, and she quickly brought her hand to her side with a slight wince. But not before Tony saw, with dawning horror, what Betty had noticed.

A growing, bright red stain on Lina's robe.

He was at her side in an instant. "Jesus, Lina! You're bleeding!"

"It's nothing, really." She shifted uncomfortably, massaging her side with one hand.

"Why didn't you say anything?" His pulse skyrocketing, he gently moved her hand aside. A tear in her robe revealed an angry slash in her spotted fur. *Wait—*

Tony blinked, certain he'd simply not parted the jagged fabric enough. But no. While he could see a glimpse of Lina's pale skin, the area surrounding her wound was all leopard.

"Lina."

"Yeah," she said haltingly, "that happens on occasion. If we're injured … during, or near, transitioning. It's not permanent. At least, not that I can remember." At his strangled sound, she squeezed his hand. "Honestly, it's not a big deal."

"Like hell it isn't. Lina, what even happened?" A horrible thought sent his own blood boiling. "Oh my god. The tranquilizer! Did they…?"

He dimly registered Opal's murmur of "Oh, shit," but had little attention for anything but his mounting panic over Lina. He bent one arm behind her knees and lifted her off the ground. She squeaked in surprise and immediately began protesting.

"We've got to get you to a doctor," he insisted.

"Tony. Tony!" Lina's command halted his movement, though it did little to soothe his agitation. She raised her hand to his face, but upon noticing the blood now streaking it, stopped shy of making contact. He let out a distressed wheeze, unable to tear his eyes from the spot.

"Look at me, Tony," Lina intoned, waiting until he did. "There is no need to panic. First of all, a doctor is the last thing I need right now." He started to argue, but Lina cocked an eyebrow and leveled him with a stern look.

A beat too late, Tony remembered the exact, *furry* nature of her injury. "Oh. But—"

"And secondly," she cut him off, "no one has been tranquilized. Do I look even remotely sleepy?"

He assessed her, taking in her vibrant hazel eyes. Feeling the hum of her magic beneath his hands. His tension began to ebb, and he shook his head.

Lina's smile reassured him further. "If you'd let me explain, I could have told you that in my rush to get to you, I scraped myself on a tree branch. This is just a scratch. That's all."

"You're sure?"

"Positive. The only thing tranquil is that tree over there." She gestured behind them, to where Ralph's lone dart lodged in the bark of an oak. Apparently Joey wasn't the only lousy shot.

"We're all safe now," Lina added.

Tony begged to differ. The tranquilizer might have missed her, but she'd still been hurt. He wanted to charge after those two jackasses and get a few punches in. Not to mention the offending tree branch, come to think of it. He'd break it into a million pieces.

He didn't realize he was growling until Lina touched his cheek. "Tony. It's fine. I'm fine."

It took him a few breaths to start to believe her. He nodded, and rested his forehead against hers.

After a few beats, she spoke. "Tony?"

"Hm?"

"Can you put me down now?"

"Oh! Sorry." He gently eased her feet back to solid ground. "We do need to get you patched up though."

Opal, who he'd nearly forgotten about, chimed in. "Why don't I take Lina back to her trailer with a first-aid kit?"

Lina nodded decisively. "Good idea."

"I'm not leaving you," he protested. "I should be the one to tend to you..."

"As much as I'd love that," Lina smiled tenderly at him, "Betty and Bob need you more than I do right now."

He opened his mouth to reply, but stopped short with a glance down at his feet. The two leopards blinked up at him, Betty in particular watching him with a near-comical mix of concern and impatience.

"Geez, I nearly forgot," he breathed. Lina cupped his cheek with her clean hand and he leaned into her caress. "My head's a mess."

"Yes. But you've definitely earned it." Her fond grin comforted him tremendously. "Get these two lovebirds secure." She paused, tilting her head in consideration. "And alert Security on the off chance those twerps decide to stop pissing themselves and come back."

He shuddered. "Absolutely." Still a bit stunned, he twisted to press his lips to her palm. "You're okay. We're okay."

"We are." She gave him a quick, fierce kiss.

Tony glanced over Lina's shoulder at Opal, who dipped her chin in reassurance. Still alarmingly calm about everything—but he'd ponder that later. At the moment, he trusted her to look after Lina while he got Betty and Bob settled.

Still in protective mode, both of them moved with Lina as she stepped away from him, and she chuckled softly. "You two are peas in a pod, just like your keeper." Placing a calming hand on each of their heads, Lina gently commanded them, "Be good for Tony now." She added conspiratorially, "And keep him from worrying too much about me, okay?"

Chapter Sixteen

*L*ina hissed as she twisted her arms to fasten her brassiere. She was glad she'd brought a spare set of underwear with her today; in the chaos of her transformation, she'd shed her robe in time, but her bra and panties were hopelessly ruined. A regrettable loss, as they'd been among her favorites.

Opal had yet to return with the first-aid kit, so Lina started cleaning her wound with a cloth and some water. And promptly hissed again. As much as it hurt, it wasn't terribly deep, which was fortunate. Stitches would have required medical assistance, and as she'd pointed out to Tony, her fur would have been awkward indeed to explain.

If memory served, magic would help it fade faster. But given her lack of practice, and the sheer volume of what she'd already expended in the last few hours, Lina felt pretty tapped out. She'd have to let mystical nature run its course and stick to human medicine for the moment.

A knock sounded on her trailer door, and Opal called out, "It's me!" before bustling in. "Okay, first-aid kit." She immediately handed Lina the tin box, then held up a small bag. "And! I found a spare robe in the Makeup trailer. If one could call it that."

Ignoring the foreboding nature of the offer, Lina thanked Opal instead. She cast a sad glance at her leopard-print robe, draped over a nearby chair. "I'm afraid mine's in sorry shape."

Opal picked it up and examined it. "Oh, this isn't too bad. A few stitches and a little hydrogen peroxide should do the trick."

Lina nodded, and busied herself with the medical supplies, while glancing at Opal in her periphery. There was no way she hadn't seen Lina transform back into herself; she'd come upon them too soon after. But she remained remarkably blasé, as if it was nothing but an everyday occurrence. Lina wasn't sure if she should be alarmed or comforted by that.

In her distraction, she forgot to steel herself against the iodine's burn. "Ow!"

Opal dropped the robe. "You okay?"

"Yep," Lina managed through gritted teeth. "Just stings a bit."

"Need any help?"

"I've got it, thanks." She waved Opal away, angling her wound toward the back of the couch, lest a flash of leopard finally trigger the woman's undoing. Lina returned to her task, unable to contain another wince.

"Once you've got everything clean," Opal said casually, "a little bit of makeup, or maybe a few dabs of putty, should cover that fur right up. I'd be happy to help … if you'd like."

She darted her eyes back to Opal, who offered her a smile. Lina huffed. "So you clocked that, did you?"

"Yeah. But the way you and Tony were whispering, I figured you didn't want to draw attention to it."

When Lina's eyebrows shot up, Opal simply shrugged.

Lina laughed. "Thanks." At Opal's nod, she added, "And I think a little gauze will do just fine." She laid a clean square over her injury, picked up a roll of tape with her free hand, then hesitated over the logistics.

"Here, let me at least do that," Opal offered, taking the tape and cutting off a few pieces.

As Lina accepted the strips and applied them in succession,

her patience began to wear thin. She took a breath before blurting, "How the hell are you so calm?"

Opal's brown eyes widened for a second, and then she laughed heartily. "I suppose I've earned that question, haven't I?" She paused. "We can get into details later, but for now… Let's just say, when it comes to the existence of the unexplained and rather … unexplainable … it's not my first lap around the pool."

While she spoke, Opal absently—or perhaps, not so absently—fiddled with the rough amethyst on a chain around her neck, a match to the one her husband, Adrian, often wore. An old, unconfirmed legend about kelpies from Lina's youth suddenly popped into her mind … along with a more recent rumor, of one who'd ventured west to live among humans. And everything snapped into place. She'd costarred with Adrian once—and couldn't believe she'd never noticed anything.

"Huh." She locked eyes with Opal, letting her grin spread. "Interesting."

Opal lifted one shoulder and grinned back. "Anyway … I'm glad you're okay. And you don't need to worry; I am a vault." She winked and started to pack up the tape and other supplies.

Lina sank back against the couch cushions with a massive sigh. *Goddesses above*, what a day. Now that she'd patched herself up, her adrenaline was wearing off—and exhaustion rushed in to take its place. Not to mention concern. She'd had a hell of a time securing Bob; though if anyone could manage two leopards at once, it was Tony.

But their close call with the circus thugs had been far too close. Goddess knew whether she and the leopards had scared them off enough for them to stay gone. Plus, even if authorities caught up to them, there was no telling whether they'd then release Bob into Tony's care. He'd worry intensely if they didn't, which would break her heart. Not to mention Betty's.

The shrill ring of a telephone startled the shit out of her. "Hell, I didn't even realize that was there. They've got the trailers wired even out here?"

"It's a pretty fancy operation," Opal replied. "Plus, this is the trailer they usually give Rex Tyler for his pictures. You wouldn't believe the perks he's got in his contract." She gestured to the still-ringing phone. "May I?"

Lina nodded in appreciation.

"Lina Leonard's trailer." Opal paused, listening. "Let me check with her." She covered the receiver with one hand. "They've got a long-distance call for you, from an apparently fierce and persistent woman named Alice? Are you up to taking it?"

Her heart lifted. "Yes, thanks."

Opal handed her the phone and gestured over her shoulder. "I'll get out of your hair and check on Tony."

"Thank you, Opal. For everything." She shared a smile with the redhead before speaking into the receiver. "I'm here, you can put the call through."

"Lina? Are you all right?" The sound of Alice's voice crackling over the line brought tears to Lina's eyes.

"Alice, hi."

"What's going on? What happened?" She sounded frantic. "My ring's been vibrating with the distress call yours put out. I've been telephoning all over town—first your place, then the studio. They're the ones who gave me this number."

Lina glanced down at her own ring in surprise. "I didn't even realize."

"Lina. What. Happened?"

She let out a sound that was half sob, half relieved laugh. "I'm not even sure where to begin." At Alice's distressed wheeze, she amended herself. "Okay, for starters, I'm safe. Everything worked out okay. I think."

Alice exhaled audibly on the other end of the line. "Thank the goddesses."

The pressure in her chest broke, and a few tears slipped free, rolling down her cheeks. "You really have no idea how good it is to hear your voice, Al."

Her friend made a sympathetic noise, which opened the

floodgates on Lina's tears and words both. Every bloody thing leading up to the events of the day tumbled out—minus a few of the more salacious details regarding herself and Tony. But she shared all the rest in a breathless rush—from him and the kittens, to her intervention with Betty, to Circus Jerk-us, as Tony called it.

When she finally finished, there was a long pause on Alice's end before she spoke.

"Fuck, Lina," she breathed. "I'm going to owe you even bigger than I thought."

That surprised a cackle out of Lina. "Well … yes."

Alice laughed along with her before sobering. "In all serious-ness, though, you're all right?" At Lina's hum of affirmation, she continued, "I'm so sorry I left you to deal with all that, hon."

Lina shivered, and realized she still wore only her underwear. She reached for Opal's bag, and pulled it open to find—

"Bloody hell."

Opal hadn't been kidding. She held up the garment in ques-tion, in all its pale pink, feather-trimmed glory. Diametrically opposed to anything she'd normally wear. She was sorely tempted to put her leopard-print one back on—torn and filthy it might be, at least it had some class.

"What is it?" Alice asked, all concern.

"Sorry, it's nothing. Only my wardrobe choices at the moment… Beggars can't be choosers, I suppose," she muttered, slipping into the feathered monstrosity against her better judge-ment. It did at least provide a touch of warmth.

"Anyway," she added, returning to more important matters. "You didn't exactly know what I was in for when you left."

"Maybe not, but still. I hate that you had to face it all alone."

"I wasn't exactly alone." The thought of Tony warmed her more than her flimsy robe, even as some of her concerns resurfaced.

"No. So tell me. This Tony chap, is he a good kisser?"

Her cheeks were fully aflame now. "Among other things…"

Alice chuckled. "Good. And … your magic is stronger around him?"

Lina straightened in her seat, wincing slightly as the bandage pulled across her cut. "It is. I didn't know it was possible. Did you?"

"I've heard things over the years; it's rare, but it does happen." She paused. "And it honestly doesn't surprise me too much."

The hair on the back of Lina's neck stood at attention. "Why's that?"

"It makes perfect sense that your magic would get stronger when your heart's inspired. You lead with your heart." Alice said it casually, completely matter-of-fact.

"I … what?"

"You lead with your heart. You always have."

Lina snorted. "That's a diplomatic way to say I'm impulsive, and exactly why the elders didn't bat an eye when I left. But what does it have to do with my magic and Tony?"

Alice was quiet for a moment, then sighed. "Okay, I should have told you this years ago, but … I had an interesting talk about you once with Sister Elizabeth. Remember her?"

"Sure, she was in charge when I left."

"Still was a couple years later, around the time you signed your first picture contract. I was so happy for you, Lina." She inhaled sharply. "But I was also a bit … sad about it."

"You never said…" Lina trailed off, slightly stunned.

"Because you'd worked so hard, and you were making your dream come true! And I really was happy for you. But … I also knew what it meant. That you were never coming back. I missed my best friend."

"Al." Her heart ached. "I wish you'd told me. I would've understood." Lina paused. "Well, I might've ranted a bit first, but I'd have gotten there eventually."

"I know," Alice said with a laugh. "Which is part of why I never said anything in the first place. Anyway, Sister Liz found me in the middle of a sulk, and was rather a good listener. At one point I asked her why they'd not fought harder to keep you from leaving. My own selfish feelings aside, I was all set to dive in and defend you."

"Thanks. I'll bet I can guess what she said…"

Alice hummed. "I wouldn't take that bet if I were you. When I asked her, straight out, if it was because of your rash tendencies, she said that was precisely why they wanted to keep you around."

"Oh, come on."

"I'm serious, Lina. It was mostly for our safety that they drilled that calm detachment into us. But Sister Liz confessed that some of the best protectors she'd ever known were the ones who jumped in with both feet, let their emotions do the guiding. Led with their hearts."

Lina's breath caught in her throat, and tears filled her eyes once more.

Alice let the revelation linger for a moment before continuing, "But everyone could see how strong your spirit was, how you were destined for something different. They couldn't have stopped you if they tried, and they didn't want to." She paused. "I still keep in touch with her, you know, and she's seen every one of your pictures. *Boneyard of Contention* was her favorite."

Lina let out a watery laugh. "I did love that one myself."

"I'm sorry I didn't tell you sooner. Truth be told, I was embarrassed. I didn't want you to think I doubted you for a second. You're living your dream, and I'm proud of you."

"Thanks," she said with a sniffle. "And yes, you should have told me. Though I get why you didn't." She hesitated, the weight of Alice's revelations, along with some questions of her own, settling on her.

"What is it?"

"Goddess, nothing gets past you, does it?" she muttered good-naturedly. "It's only… I'm fucking exhausted, Alice." Her shoulders sagged with the admission. "Today was impossible, on top of everything the last few weeks. Sure, I helped scare those creeps away, but there was so much I *didn't* get right. And as wonderful as it's been to reconnect with this part of me, I still don't want this life. I don't think I'd survive doing all this on a regular basis."

Alice's melodic laugh startled her. "Well, of course not. Who said you had to?"

"I…"

"Lina. It doesn't have to be all or nothing. Use your magic when, or *if*, you want to. And if that only includes standing in for your leopard friends on occasion and enjoying some quality frisky time with your gentleman friend," she said with another laugh, "then so be it. You don't need to be so dramatic about it. Goddess knows, you sure picked the right profession there."

Lina joined in her laughter, her heart feeling lighter than it had in ages. "Thank you, Al."

"Anytime, darling."

The trailer door suddenly burst open. "Lina! You wouldn't believe—" Tony stopped short when he saw the telephone in her hand. "Oh, sorry. I can come back…" He gestured behind him.

She put a hand over the mouthpiece. "No, don't. It's Alice."

He nodded, his expression an odd mix of relief and concern. Lina belatedly realized the evidence of her tears must be all over her face. She was about to reassure him when Alice's voice reached her through the phone.

"Do you love him, Lina?"

"What?"

Despite her surprise, as she stared at Tony, the answer to Alice's question wove its way through her bloodstream, calling to her magic with every beat of her heart.

"I do," she whispered.

"Then the rest will sort itself out." She could hear Alice's smile in her voice. "I'll let you get back to him. But I'm taking the next train back to Los Angeles. And don't even think to argue! I want to see for myself that you're all right. And meet this Tony fella."

Lina chuckled. "Deal."

"I love you, Li."

"Love you, too."

The instant Lina replaced the phone in its cradle, Tony knelt at her side and brushed a stray tear from her cheek. "Are you okay?"

"I'm even better now." At his warm, but still solicitous, smile, she added, "Alice called to check on me, and things took a wee serious turn. But a good one, really."

She raked her hand through his hair and took in his dear, dear face. She wanted to know what had kept him, and how Betty and Bob fared. But her conversation with Alice, especially its end, had her mind reeling.

Her heart was louder and more insistent.

Lina pulled Tony's mouth to hers. He kissed her back hungrily, both of them pouring their relief and gratitude and passion into each other. She could have gone on kissing him for hours, but when his hand skimmed over her waist and accidentally brushed over her bandaged cut, her audible wince pulled them back to the present.

He raised anguished eyes to her. "Oh god, I'm sorry, Lina. Did I hurt you?"

She shook her head. "You startled me more than anything."

Tony's hand hovered over her side without actually touching her. "You're sure you're not hurt badly?"

"Positive. The iodine hurt more than the cut itself."

His face melted, before quickly twisting in a grimace. He rubbed at his nose, and Lina suspected he might be on the verge of a sneeze, but he stifled it. Glancing down at her, he asked, "What *are* you wearing?"

Lina bit back a laugh. "A spare Opal had in her trailer. I know, it's awful."

"I'll say. Speaking of Opal… How much did she see? Is she…?"

"She saw plenty, but don't worry, she'll be fine." Lina chuckled. "I'll let her tell you why."

He raised his eyebrows in clear intrigue, but the reminder of what had transpired in the woods pushed aside Lina's levity, ushering back some of her earlier concerns. "But enough about me and Opal. You had things to tell me when you came in? Are Betty and Bob all right?"

Tony's answering grin was the best thing she'd ever seen. "Lina, it worked out so much better than I could've hoped." He settled himself on the floor and took her hands in his. "I got Betty and Bob settled in her pen pretty quickly. Poor things were pretty wiped out; they snuggled up and dozed right off."

"Aw."

"I still can't believe she's got a boyfriend…" He shook his head. "Anyway, I'd no sooner headed out to find someone from Security when a guard found me first. He wanted to make sure we were okay. Turns out, they were already on top of the Ralph and Joey situation because … get this … the cops tipped them off. They'd been following those clowns all day, and nabbed them as soon as they ran away from us!"

"You're joking! How? Why?"

He huffed. "You would not believe the shit those guys have been up to. The fuzz across three counties have been staking them out for months, building up one hell of a case. They got extra suspicious when Ralph and Joey headed up here, so they followed."

"Smart move." With a smirk, she added, "Maybe you should've gone with your anonymous tip idea after all."

"I doubt I could have been half as creative as the truth. Gambling rings, roving pickpockets. Turns out Bob was their star attraction because he was the cover for a floating crap game."

"Damn." A devastating prospect occurred to her. "They didn't deliberately hurt him, did they?"

Tony shook his head soberly. "No, thank god. He was important to them, so they treated him pretty well. The injury that brought him to us was, indeed, likely an accident. And given how close the cops were watching, I'm sure they would've moved in sooner if they'd seen evidence of violence."

"That's a relief. Yet how did they not move in, let alone seem to notice, when an entire leopard got loose?"

He snorted. "God only knows. I still have no idea how Bob managed it."

"So what happens now?"

"That's the best part. Security brought one of the officers over, and I filled him in on the run-in we had. Not that they needed more evidence, but it'll go on the laundry list of charges, once they take our official statements. I convinced the officer Ralph and Joey must've been mistaken, or lying, about a third leopard too." Tony winked, even as he vibrated with excitement. "And ... he agreed that Applegate is the best place to take Bob until everything gets sorted."

"Tony, that's wonderful."

"I'm pretty sure I can convince them to let us keep him long-term. There'll be mountains of paperwork to get through, but we're easily the best solution."

"Of course you are." Lina gave him a quick kiss. "Wait. What about the screen test?" She braced herself to get up, but Tony stilled her with a gentle hand on her knee.

"Peabody called the rest of it off. He's livid that danger was allowed to befall his star, and almost as angry over my being at risk. Or maybe it was more for Betty, but hey, I'll take it. He assured me they got enough footage before all hell broke loose, and we should all get some rest."

Hope bloomed in her chest. "And they'll give you and Betty the job, right? There's never been a doubt about your talent, but now that you add the sympathy angle..."

He beamed. "Peabody practically said as much." With a snort, he added, "You should've seen him when he saw both leopards, head swiveling like a dervish. Although ... once he recovered, he was eyeing Bob pretty hungrily. I feel sorry for that screenwriter. You might end up starring opposite two cats now."

They snickered. Lina ran her fingers through Tony's ginger waves again, reveling in his contented sigh.

"I'm so happy you're safe," Tony breathed, at the same time Lina spoke.

"I was so scared when I heard you with those goons."

Their mingled laughter deepened, even as the gravity of all they'd just faced, and survived, settled in.

She'd believed the assurances she gave Tony in her pep talks, but goddesses above, it was something else to know she'd been right. They were safe. Together. And employed on top of it all. She sank back against the couch cushions, her exhaustion returning with a vengeance.

"I think I've used more magic today than I have in the last fifteen years combined."

"You were magnificent back there," Tony said softly.

She felt her cheeks flush. "I have to admit, it was great fun making those knuckleheads piss themselves. Though I thought we were cooked when Bob first showed up."

"I've never seen anyone run so fast." He snorted. "I even worried I might be losing it myself for a minute there."

"I am sorry about that. If I'd tied him up tighter…"

"There was no stopping Bob when it came to Betty. Believe me, if I'd sensed you in danger, no rope could've held me either." His lopsided grin eased her mind and made her stomach swoop. "I assume you used some of your powers on him?"

"Yes. Put him to sleep, and then tried to hide him with some glamouring." She grimaced. "Guess I was oh-for-two."

His snicker quickly escalated into full laughter. "It was unbelievable, the way he kept … flickering in and out. I thought Joey's head was going to explode."

Lina wished she could find the humor in it as well, but the memory of her earlier fear for Tony and the leopards kept it at bay. She buried her face in her hands with a groan.

"Hey." Tony gently tugged her wrists, waiting until she lowered her hands and looked at him. He studied her for a long moment. "What is it?"

"I should've done a better job securing him in the first place. I ended up putting him in danger too."

"Lina, those guys were about to take not only Betty, but *you*. As fierce as you were, they had that damn tranq gun. If Bob hadn't shown up when he did, and in the state he was in…" He shivered. "I don't even want to think about it."

"I know. Still…"

"I'm supposed to be the worrywart in this pair, remember?" His warm brown eyes were full of concern. "What's really going on?"

Her conversation with Alice came flooding back—not only the reassurances, but all of Lina's doubts in the first place. *It doesn't have to be all or nothing.* But would Tony understand that? He was so impressed with what she'd done…

She debated how much to reveal, but her desire to be honest with him won out. "Today was … a lot. Yes, a few parts of it were fun. And I would absolutely jump in to save you, and those leopards, again. Every time. But…" She paused, and then the words cascaded out of her. "It almost didn't work. And everything that happened today, starting with Bob, *especially* with Bob, reminded me of all the reasons I left this life, this part of me. I'm out of practice, and it took so much out of me. To the point that my magic didn't hold."

She didn't realize a few tears had escaped until Tony reached up to brush one off her cheek.

"It has been wonderful reconnecting with that side of myself." She brushed her fingers over his jaw. "And I do love the way my magic comes to life when I'm with you. Now that I've found it again, I don't want to give it up entirely."

"But you don't want to suddenly become Alice, either."

"No. You and I make a great team, and we've done a lot of good for those leopards, but … I'm an actress. And I can't go through a day like today on a regular basis."

"Of course you can't. Neither can I." He exhaled sharply. "God, I hope I *never* have a day like this again. You know better than anyone what a wreck I've been lately. I'm beyond ready to go back to helping animals in the most boring ways possible."

Lina allowed herself a laugh. "You'd better make sure Gouda knows that."

"Duly noted." His expression, while remaining warm, took on a serious edge. "Lina, are you worried that if you're not always using your magic to help me out of scrapes, I'll be disappointed?"

She stared at him, unsure why his insight surprised her. "I... Yes. I know it's silly, but..."

"It's not silly. But it's also... Okay, it's a little silly."

At her half-amused, half-affronted sigh, he grinned and lifted onto his knees, his face close to hers.

"I've said a version of this before, but I'm going to say it again, because you clearly need to hear it." He took her hands in a firm grip, his thumbs rubbing soothing circles. "Lina, you know I don't care about you because you're a movie star, but I also don't care about you because of your magic. Yes, it's an extraordinarily impressive part of you, but it's just that—*part* of you. I started falling before I knew anything about it, and I care ... I *love* you for who you are. For all of you."

Lina's breath stuttered out. "Tony..."

He tucked her hair behind her ear, his hand lingering to caress her cheek. "Lina, I love you. Because you make me laugh. You share my taste in pulp fiction. You don't seem to mind that I keep serving you cold food. You know exactly how to talk me down from Catastrophe Mountain, and call me out on my bullshit when I go too far." He feathered a kiss over her knuckles. "You haven't used your magic in *fifteen* years, yet you brought it out of retirement, at tremendous risk to yourself, to help a lovesick leopard ... and her lovesick minder."

Her watery laugh made him smile. "I think you are magnificent, Lina Leonard. Simply because you're *you*." He shook his head. "And the biggest miracle of all is that somehow, you seem to want me."

"I don't just want you," she corrected him. "I love you, too, Tony. So very much."

His grin nearly blinded her. "Yeah?"

"Hell yeah." She brushed a stray ginger lock off his forehead. "Alice has a theory that my magic responds so strongly to you because I lead with my heart. And she's right. My heart's been responding to you practically since the first."

"When I yelled at you for scattering my kittens?"

She laughed. "When you cared so much for your kittens that you didn't want to see harm come to them. I love how deeply you care for all your animals, the way you feel *everything* so deeply. The way you let me step in to help, even when you didn't understand it all. Your taste in books, your cold food, even your terribly inappropriate—but awfully sweet—apology meat."

"Hey!" He chuckled.

"I'm happy with the life I created. I love what I do. But I don't think I realized just how isolated I kept myself, never letting people get too close. Letting you in, being part of a team—and a damn good one, at that—it's everything, Tony." She grinned, parroting his words back to him. "And that's because you're you."

He leaned forward and captured her mouth. The soft perfection of his lips, the heat of his tongue sliding against hers... Her last, lingering worries faded into nothingness, and her spent reserve of magic tingled to life once more.

Tony broke their kiss and rested his forehead against hers, the warmth of his exhale whispering over her skin.

"Lina, I love the team we've started to create, and I can't wait to fall even harder for you under completely mundane circumstances. I want nothing more than to see how uneventful we can make our lives." She chuckled, but he wasn't finished. "If you'll let me, I plan to spend every day making sure I keep earning your trust, your love. Being the best partner I can be to you."

"While keeping the leopard's share of our excitement in the bedroom?"

He snickered, then stole her breath when his eyes darkened with heat. "You better believe it, kitten," he rasped.

"That sounds absolutely…" She recovered enough to smirk. "…*purrfect.*"

Tony broke their contact to throw his head back on a laugh, which she readily joined. He glanced down at her with a wince. "Really, though. That robe has got to go."

She held his molten gaze as she parted the garment and slid it off her shoulders, as seductively as she could manage with such a feathery monstrosity. Once free, she pulled him closer for another kiss, and they devoured each other's resulting groans. Remaining ever careful of the wound she'd nearly forgotten, he rose over her and eased her back against the couch gently, while his mouth remained anything but. She matched him stroke-for-stroke and let her hands go wild in his hair.

It might have been her magic, or simply *their* magic, but her entire body lit with sparks. She loved this man, and he loved her. And hell, even their leopards were going to get a happily ever after. Her heart had never felt so full.

Lina lost track of time as their kisses melted on and on. Tony trailed his lips over her jaw, and she dimly noted a scratching sound somewhere outside, then forgot it entirely when he took her earlobe in a gentle nip. The trail of fire he blazed down her throat left her purring, but he stopped all too soon.

"Do you hear that?" he asked against her collarbone.

"Just a tree branch or something." She tugged his hair, and he came willingly back to her mouth.

"Lina…" He froze. "Okay, really, what *is* that?"

Much to her dismay, the scritch grew louder, and thus harder to ignore. "Come to think of it, it's not windy today, certainly not enough to move the trees that much."

"It's too quiet to be someone knocking. Probably nothing, right?"

"Absolutely."

He nodded, and they attempted further kissing—to no avail. *Dammit.* Not only did the scratching get more insistent—it was punctuated by a few small thuds.

Tony heaved a sigh. "I have to go see who, or what, is out there. Don't I?"

"I guess so."

He stood stiffly, what with his lovely erection, and then surprised her with a quick kiss on the tip of her nose. He pointed at her. "Do not move."

With a smile, she mimed a clawing motion with her hand. "Cat's honor."

His laugh echoed through the trailer as he moved to open the door and peer out. "I don't see any—" His words cut off, and his breath hitched audibly. "Oh, come on!"

She sat up. "What is it?"

"It's not possible," he muttered, bending down.

Before she could question him further, he straightened and turned to face her—with Gouda in his arms.

Lina gasped. "How in the hell did she get here?"

"I have no fucking clue. She must've stowed away in my truck this morning."

"Or…" She bit her lip, and he looked at her quizzically. "Maybe my earlier theory about Bob's great escape … wasn't such a fantastic theory after all?"

Tony pulled a face as he sat next to her. "No. That isn't… I mean…"

He lifted Gouda to eye level, and they both analyzed her for a long moment. The kitten responded with a tiny—and rather indignant—meow. Lina and Tony stared at each other in disbelief. And then burst into laughter.

He slumped against the cushions with a groan, still holding the cat aloft. "Gouda, what am I going to do with you?"

Lina nudged his shoulder with her own. "What are *we* going to do with you?"

His answering grin could have lit up the entire city. Gouda, to her credit, didn't protest when Lina and Tony leaned in to seal their agreement with a kiss.

Epilogue

One Year Later

Tony glanced up at the red light over the soundstage door, and finding it off, deemed it safe to enter. He opened the door with caution anyway, just in case, but the coast was more than clear. It was the final day of filming on Lina's current picture, the wrap party already in full swing. Actors and crew members mingled on the set, and a few tables had been set up with refreshments.

He zeroed in on Lina immediately, and his breath caught, as it always did. They'd been married a few weeks now, and he thanked his lucky stars every day that he got to share his life with her.

When Lina spotted him, her face lit up. He thought he might levitate right off the floor as he made a beeline for her.

"What are you doing here?" She greeted him with a quick kiss.

"Carl is checking on a patient nearby, so I had him drop me off. I thought I'd surprise you, and then we could head home together."

Her dark red lips curved in that smile he so treasured. "My kind of surprise. And your timing is perfect. This shindig's starting to wind down." She lifted the small plate in her hand. "Want some cheesecake?"

"Ooh, the kind they serve in the commissary? The one that has no business being as delicious as it is?"

"You bet. Here." She lifted a forkful, offering to feed him, her eyes dancing with mischief.

He made an exaggerated show of taking the bite, reveling in the way she stared hungrily at his mouth. Unable to resist teasing her further, he lingered over licking the last of it off his bottom lip. Her quiet purr made him chuckle.

She glanced around the room, cheeks flushing prettily. "You're impossible, you know that?"

"What?" He shrugged, not-so-innocently.

"Let's get out of here."

Tony trailed beside Lina as she made a quick circuit of the room to express her thanks and goodbyes, offering his own greetings to a few of the faces he knew. They finally emerged, arm-in-arm, into the late afternoon sunlight, and had only taken a few steps when they ran into Nick Bradley, complete with a ginger cat in his arms.

"Lina, Tony, hello!" Nick grinned as he took in Tony's expression, and gestured at the cat. "Don't worry, this isn't one of yours."

Tony laughed. "I'll admit, I was worried there for a second."

"So who is this regal lass?" Lina asked.

"This is Lady Macbeth." Nick gave the cat an affectionate rub before leaning toward them conspiratorially. "If we're being honest, I think she's been a little put-out over all the cats, and leopards, we've had on the lot over the last year. I figured I'd bring her to work with me, let her know she's still number one in my heart. After Lois, of course."

Lina nodded in approval. "You're a wise man."

Lady M let out a haughty meow, then snuggled adorably against Nick, making them all laugh.

"So are you finished already?" Nick asked Lina. "I was just on my way to your wrap party."

"Afraid so. Although there's plenty of party left to be had." Her fingers tightened on Tony's arm. "But this gent and I are headed home."

Nick grinned. "Well, don't let me hold you up. Congrats on the picture, which I'm hearing great things about, and again, on your wedding. Take all the time you need on that trip," he added with a wink.

They'd put off their honeymoon until Lina finished filming, and were departing for Ireland in a few days.

"Thanks, Nick," Lina said.

Tony pointed at Lady M. "Luckily for you, our absence means you've got lots of time to make things up to this gal." After Betty's movie debut, the studio had kept Tony plenty busy, throwing a few more animal pictures his way—not to mention some generous donations for the sanctuary.

"I plan to take full advantage," Nick assured him. "Bon voyage!"

They parted ways amiably. But as they headed for Lina's trailer, the reminder of their upcoming trip reawakened a concern that had been gnawing at Tony all day.

Of course, Lina noticed.

"Everything okay?" she asked. "You're not worried the Char-cat-erie will sense Lady Macbeth's essence on you and get jealous themselves?"

Her nickname for the kittens never failed to make him snicker. "No, I'm sure they can handle it. If anything, they'd be eager to meet her and try to impress her. Though we should probably keep Muenster away. He's turning into quite the little rake."

Lina's chuckle was delectably husky. "Good idea. That empress is far too much woman for him." His own laugh faded when she squeezed his arm. "But don't distract me. What's going on?"

"Nothing, really. I'm probably being silly."

"But…?"

"I heard a rather alarming sound this morning."

Lina stopped in front of her trailer with a mock pout. "Excuse me. I thought you loved all my noises."

"I do." He bent to growl in her ear, "As a matter of fact, I'm looking forward to eliciting every single one of them, all the way across this continent, and then the Atlantic." Her resulting shiver made him half-hard already, despite their surroundings. "And who's distracting whom now?"

"Just making sure," she purred, with a pinch to his ass that made him laugh. "Come on." She ushered them into her dressing room. "So … this noise?"

"Right. I think it was Betty. Followed by Bob." He gave her a pointed look.

Lina's eyebrows shot up. "Oh. You think they're ready to start trying again?"

The previous year, once all the dust cleared from their adventures and Bob settled into his new home, the leopards had indeed become a couple. Complete with mating. *So. Much. Mating.* Applegate had become one hell of an awkward place to be.

Interestingly enough, all that action—really, he had no idea how they'd sustained it—hadn't resulted in any cubs, as he'd thought it would. Not that Betty and Bob seemed to mind. Once they finally paused their efforts, they'd taken the Char-cat-erie under their wing and quasi-adopted the lot of them. Bob, in particular, was surprisingly gentle and patient with the small, rowdy bunch.

As evidenced by the framed photo hanging next to Lina's mirror, which always made Tony smile. Alice had gifted them a session with a portrait photographer, and the results were perfection. Betty and Bob sat patiently on their haunches, looking dapper—Betty in a rhinestone collar, a gift from Lina; and Bob in the elegant black bow tie Tony had found him. The seven kittens surrounded them, being their usual chaotic selves. Tony loved everything about the picture, but his favorite part had to be Bob's majestic expression, in spite of Gouda lounging atop his head like a furry crown. They'd become an adorable little family.

Needless to say, the all-too-familiar mating calls he'd heard that morning caught him off guard.

"It sure sounded like it," Tony admitted to Lina. "And I'm happy for them, really. It's a bit of a relief to know they're still bonded that way, and not getting tired of each other."

Lina grinned at him. "I knew you were a romantic deep down, Tony Benson. So ... what's the problem?"

"It's the timing. Should we really be leaving right now?"

"We should absolutely make our escape." She folded her arms across her chest. "Have you forgotten what they were like last time?"

Tony shuddered. "I don't think I'll ever forget, as long as I live. But that's just it. We'll be gone for a whole month. What are we leaving Carl, and especially Alice, to deal with? She was generous enough to offer to stay at Applegate while we're gone. I know she's still trying to make it up to you for last year, but I'd hate for her to think we're intentionally subjecting her to..."

"Relentless leopard-fucking. Multiple times a day. For weeks on end. It really was a lot, wasn't it?" She blew out a breath. "I see your point. But I'm sure Alice will be fine. We can give her fair warning."

"Is there such a thing?"

"We'll do our best."

"If you say so."

She snaked her arms around his neck, and he pulled her close. He didn't think he'd ever get over how perfect she felt in his arms. Or how much she eased even his smallest troubles.

"Besides," she said, "we need to go on this trip now."

"Why's that?"

She hesitated, a flash of doubt crossing her expression.

"Because if we don't do it soon, I'm liable to lose my nerve altogether."

"Lina." He cursed himself for not noticing her own worries sooner. "We can wait, if you…"

"No. I want to. Truly. I'm just a little nervous, is all." She offered him a small smile.

They'd settled on Ireland for their honeymoon in part because he'd never been there. She wanted to give him the grand tour of where she'd grown up and show him off to her family. The family she hadn't seen in years.

Lina was still reacquainting herself with her magic—using it on occasion with their cats, big and small, mostly for fun—and she'd opened up more with Alice. Tony could see how much unexpected joy it brought her to share that long-buried side of herself.

"I'm sure they'll be thrilled to see you," he reassured her now. "Alice said they're excited."

"I know. And I am excited too. I've missed my family. It's just been so long … I feel like such a different person now."

"An extraordinary person, and don't you forget it." He kissed her forehead. "Really, though, if you're not ready, we can go another time. I'll brave the leopard orgy."

Lina snickered. "Thank you, darling." She sighed. "But I'm ready. It's time I go back. No more *all-or-nothing*." Her fingers tangled in the hair above his collar, and her smile brightened. "You have no idea how it feels to be myself, all of myself, with you. Thank you for being my safe space."

Tony's eyes misted. "Thank you for being mine. You make me feel pretty invincible, you know."

"I love you."

"I love you, too." He kissed her, deep and slow, pouring every bit of himself into it, savoring all she gave him. Too soon, she pulled away with a groan.

"Come on, let's go home. We still have loads of packing to do.

And it's going to take us twice as long to make sure Gouda doesn't stow away in our luggage."

"Ugh, you're right. The last thing we need is her causing an incident in international waters."

"Oh, I nearly forgot!" Lina retrieved a parcel wrapped in brown paper from her dressing table. "I was hoping this would arrive in time for the wedding, but now it'll give us some reading material for the trip."

He took the package from her and unwrapped it. It was a gently used paperback, and he let out a bark of laughter at the title. "*Miss Corker Meets a New Yorker*? You're kidding me! Did you have the prop department make this one up?"

She huffed in affront. "I most certainly did not. It's real. And very rare, apparently, this elusive third cousin."

"My apologies." He grinned at his wife. "It's absolutely perfect. Thank you, kitten. I have to admit, though, I'm not sure I can wait till we're on the road to start it. We might have to settle into bed with it tonight."

Her contented purr was everything. "I was hoping you'd say that."

As they gathered her things, their laughter mingled, lingering all the way home to the loft they now shared. They might be about to embark on an international trip, but Lina Leonard was all the adventure he'd ever need.

Acknowledgments

Thank you so much, dear readers, for returning to the Phoenix Pictures Vault with me. I hope you enjoyed Lina and Tony's love story, and their many adventures with their feline friends. And thank you for indulging me as I lived vicariously through my characters—sadly, my lifelong allergy has been at war with my lifelong love of cats, but at least I can spend quality time with them on the page! On that note, I am also eternally grateful to one of the truly best things to come of the internet: cat videos and memes. They made for excellent "research" as I wrote this novella.

I'd also like to extend a special thanks to the reference librarians at the Academy of Motion Picture Arts & Sciences for pointing me in the direction of the National Park Service, and Mike, formerly of the NPS, whose research on the history of Paramount Ranch was invaluable in helping me confirm a rather random detail. Namely, the possibility of Lina receiving a phone call in her trailer at my fictional Ransom Ranch. At least some buildings on a property like that would have indeed been wired for telephones in 1949— any creative license about whether they'd extend to individual trailers is strictly my own.

As always, my writing journey would absolutely not be the same without my Sploosh Sisters, my wonderful group of critique partners and friends. Amanda Pereira, Jillian Graves, Daria Vernon, and Genevieve Kersten—you are simply the best.

Big thanks to Carla for your feedback and excitement for my Phoenix universe, and for your friendship! And to all my friends and family, thank you for your unending support.

To my fantastic editor, Michele Chiappetta, thank you again for all your feedback, and for helping my words be the best they can be. It's always such a delight to work with you.

The stunning illustration gracing the cover of this book is the artwork of Yulia Yemelianova (who also knocked it out of the park for *Sea Creatures Prefer Redheads*). I had a wonderful time partnering with you again—and I always know that my characters' hands are in excellent hands with your artistic vision! Thank you.

Thanks as always to my dad, for your support and encouragement and...everything. And of course, to my mom—I miss you every day. I'm so grateful I can channel my love of the classic screwball comedies you introduced me to into my writing —and in this case, one of our favorites, *Bringing Up Baby*.

And finally, once again, thank you, readers. Knowing that there are people who are enjoying my stories, understanding what I'm trying to say with them, and falling in love with the characters who mean so much to me, is everything.

Also by Brianne Gillen

The Phoenix Pictures Series:

DIFFICULT

SINGLE INDEMNITY

A KISS TO BUILD A GRUDGE ON

First Harvest of Love: A Lughnasadh Short Story

(Newsletter exclusive)

From the Phoenix Pictures Vault:

SEA CREATURES PREFER REDHEADS (novella)

MY FAVORITE LEOPARD (novella)

***

Did you enjoy this book? Please consider leaving a review!

…on Goodreads, Bookbub, or your retailer of choice

About the Author

Brianne Gillen is a romance author, costume designer, theatre educator, and life-long storyteller, based in the Los Angeles area. She loves classic films, especially the screwball comedies of the '30s and '40s, and will never turn down the opportunity to browse the treasure troves otherwise known as vintage clothing stores. She is also a voracious reader and firm believer in happily-ever-afters. She has done a bit of playwriting, and in recent years, has contributed her opinions to a few online publications centering on the art and craft of costume design. Her Phoenix Pictures Series centers around fierce dames and cinnamon-roll gents finding love in late-1940s Hollywood.

www.briannegillen.com

 instagram.com/booksbybrianne
 x.com/BooksbyBrianne

www.ingramcontent.com/pod-product-compliance
Lightning Source LLC
Chambersburg PA
CBHW030943210726
48290CB00007B/2303